Landfall Volume 1 Survival

Vic Broquard

Landfall – Volume 1 –Survival
First Edition

ISBN: 978-1-941415-91-7

Published by:
http://www.Broquard-ebooks.com
Broquard eBooks
1055 Brandy Lake Rd
Woodruff, WI 54568
author@Broquard-eBooks.com

For Morgan and L. Ron Hubbard

Table of Contents

Chapter 1 Preparations

Security escorted the English liaison, Miss Raven Cooper, to the Hawker's bridge, a cigar-shaped heavy cruiser. The twenty-two-year-old woman anticipated Commander Bloom's recognition, but instead he demanded the bridge crew's attention.

Streaks of gray contrasted with the commander's anger. "I can't believe it! The Hawker used as a livestock transport! In all my years, I've never seen a heavy cruiser so abused. Preposterous!"

His XO, Faith Kay Koralsky, straightened her uniform before responding. "I know, sir. And with the impending war with the Imperium expected any day..."

"Right! And we are long overdue for that major retrofit. We need better everything."

"Right, sir. Remember? That's why we need this milk run. This two-hour transport to New Terra for Billionaire Stroebel finances the ship's entire retrofit. Besides, it's only a two-hour flight to New Terra. We'll be in maintenance before supper. How long do you think the retrofit will take? Don't want to miss fleet launch." She smiled, as the red vanished from the man's cheeks. "Besides, we can visit the sights of Paris."

Anger defused, the crew returned to its duties.

That's a good move, Raven thought. *She's the actual commander here.*

Commander Bloom said, "The upgrade should take about a week. We'll use that time to train the new crew of a thousand plus and five hundred Marines waiting for us. Then, we can kick ass, XO. Just try to run a heavy cruiser with this skeleton crew. Almost impossible."

"But reducing our crew increased our cargo load by 30%," XO Koralsky said. "Twenty-four of us, sir; more than enough for this two-hour milk run."

"Aye, once we get those infernal animals loaded."

Raven shifted her weight, getting the security man's attention.

He cleared his throat. "Commander, the English liaison and her group have arrived. Permission to begin boarding?"

"Granted." He turned to his XO. "God, you handle these people and their animals. I want nothing to do with it. How the hell will we ever get the stench out of my ship?"

"Glad that's maintenance people's job, not ours, sir."

As Commander Bloom stomped off the bridge, grins shot her way from the other bridge staff. His fading footsteps echoed throughout the empty halls. Raven noticed the man in the pilot's chair winking at Koralsky.

"At ease, everyone," the XO said, before drilling her eyes onto Raven, who had penetrating blue eyes and long black hair.

"Raven Cooper, ma'am. I'm the liaison for the English group of five hundred seventy-five. We're transporting hundreds of crated chickens and geese."

"Follow me. I'll show you to your quarters. Captain, escort her group to Hold One. After they stow their cargo, show them to cabins on Deck 1. This way, Raven."

"Should I present myself to Commander Bloom?"

"Ah, you don't really want to do that. He's in a foul mood. He's not pleased with his Hawker becoming a barnyard."

Ravel grinned. "I can imagine. This was our last chance to leave Earth before the war begins. We had to take it. As I understand it, German billionaire Jan Stroebel made this possible by making Space Command an offer they couldn't refuse. Can't argue with money."

"Lord knows how badly the Hawker needs a retrofit."

"Good job defusing the commander's furry."

Faith smiled. "So why are you moving to this new world, New Terra? If you don't mind me asking? The war? We could always use more women in the Space Force."

"Me? I just got my physics degree, and they offered

me a teaching job on New Terra that I couldn't turn down. Earth's going to be a prime target in the looming war. So my folks moved to Empress Parkinson's Paradise 2 world. But there are too many genetic mutants there for my liking. I want to make a difference. This seemed like the right opportunity. To teach young minds how things work."

"Makes sense. So, you're also a chicken farmer?"

Raven laughed. "Hardly. No, that's Dusty Baker's thing. They elected me spokesperson because of my degree. She's rounded up like-minded from the US and England. And she's bringing hundreds of the birds with her. Some are egg layers, but some are better as food. Not my area of eggs-pertise."

Faith rolled her eyes, but grinned.

"This is your quarters. You're free to roam the ship, just not on the bridge. There's the intercom if you need something."

"I should go meet the other leaders as they arrive."

***

An hour later, Raven waited at the loading ramp as Jan Stroebel led the German group up to the ship. XO Koralsky moved to Raven's side.

"You must be Herr Stroebel. I'm XO Faith Kay Koralsky. On behalf of the commander and crew of the Hawker, we thank you for your generous financial contribution."

Not even the tiniest dust particle resided on his black suit. The rotund man straightened his suit coat.

"I expected Commander Broom to meet us."

"Bloom, sir," the XO said.

Money doesn't equal brains, Raven thought.

"The world doesn't revolve around you, Dad," sixteen-year-old Hanna Stroebel said, momentarily glancing up from her phone. "Can't we stay here? We don't wanna move. We're losing all our friends. You can't do this to us!"

Her younger brother, Bart, continued playing a game on his phone.

"Shut up. Ignore her. I'm afraid I've spoiled both kids. They don't have a clue how the world operates. We're bringing mining gear with us, as specified."

"As long as it doesn't exceed the weight limits," Faith said. "Welcome. I'll show you to your quarters and then to meet Commander Bloom, sir."

"Ah, Miss Raven Cooper. I trust you've handled the English group?"

"Yes, all stowed and ready for takeoff. Again, we can't thank you enough for your generosity."

He nodded.

Hanna rolled her eyes. "Whatever."

"Be civil, Hanna. Lead on, XO. Liaison Cooper, join us. I want to discuss some last-minute ideas with you and the other liaisons."

As they walked, Raven dropped back to Hanna's side since Herr Stroebel forgot about her. "Isn't your mother coming?"

"You kidding? She died when I was five. Dad always gets what he wants. God knows why he wants us kids. We sure don't want him."

"You don't want to move to New Terra?"

"Hardly. Don't know anyone there. Don't want to lose my friends. Tried to burn our mansion down to make him leave us."

Bart spoke up. "Told you that wouldn't work. Just go along with him for a couple of years. When you're eighteen, you can do what you want."

"But I want to do that now. Who wants to move to some world with no people on it?"

Raven said, "I've heard this world has lots of kids your ages. I might be your physics teacher."

"Whatever..." Hanna refused to look up from her phone, sending a last text message before departure.

Having shown them their quarters, Faith led Herr Stroebel and Raven to the commander's quarters. "Commander, this is Herr Stroebel. Commander Bloom."

"So good finally to meet you, Herr Stroebel. On behalf of the entire Hawker, we cannot thank you enough for your timely generosity," the commander said, vigorously shaking hands. "That'll be all, XO, Raven."

Faith and Raven headed back to the cargo hold. Faith said, "Commander Bloom sure can hobnob with the wealthy. Better him than me."

"Herr Stroebel has a temper," Raven said. "Just hope he holds it together until we get there. I liked how you defused the situation on the bridge."

Once the crew loaded the heavier equipment, the Spanish group arrived. Raven and Faith met them.

"My counterpart. Liaison Rafael Ortiz," Raven said. "The Hawker XO, Faith Kay Koralsky."

The young man kissed Faith's hand. "So pleased to meet you."

Retracting her hand, Faith said, "I understand you're loading horses?"

"*Sí.* One hundred fifty of the finest. Do not worry. Our vet has given them something to keep them calm for the trip. If you'll show us where to bring them..."

Raven grinned, noticing Rafael's failure to charm the pants off the XO.

"I'll take you to your quarters, Mr. Ortiz," Faith said, "and then to meet Commander Bloom."

"Oh, I don't need to meet him. I'd love to have you show me around your powerful ship. Perhaps share lunch with me later? If your duties permit..."

Raven grinned as Faith ignored him.

With the horses secured, Raven and Faith met the Scottish liaison, Bain Macnab, and his family, all fiery redheads.

He said, "So pleased to meet you, XO Koralsky. My wife, Bonnie, and our children: Fiona and Dave."

"Likewise. Say, after I show you to your cabin, perhaps Fiona and Dave would like to meet Herr Stroebel's two teens. They are about your ages," Faith said.

"Could we, Dad?" Fiona said.

"Of course. I know we're taking you away from your friends, but I told you there would be lots of new ones to make."

After showing them their cabin, Raven whispered to Faith. "Smart move with the kids."

She whispered back. "I was once young, too. Kind of interesting seeing all those sheep herding dogs."

"Border collies," Raven said.

When they returned to the entrance, the odor of hundreds of sheep overpowered them.

Faith said, "Now I know why Commander Bloom assigned me greet duties."

"I think it'll soon be worse. Here comes the last group, the Basque people," Raven said. "Hi, Zigor. Zigor Ugarte, this is the Hawker XO Faith Kay Koralsky."

After exchanging greetings, he said, "Two hundred cattle and fifty milkers, as agreed. Our vet, Mirari, has given them something to keep them calm, especially the bulls."

His black hair mirrored Raven's, but his pale skin stood out from the olive-colored Spaniards. He stood four inches taller than Raven and Faith. He had a flattened nose.

"So, why are you moving? I thought you Basque would never leave your land," Faith asked as she and Raven led his family to their quarters.

"Most of the others are leaving because Earth's overrun with all these immigrants from Federation over-populated worlds. Just dumped them on Earth. Suppose they had to do that, what with the corporations sending most of Earth's people to colonize all the new worlds the Sol Empire has discovered. That and the coming war. Us? We don't really want to move, but with all the disasters caused by all these alien immigrants who don't give a donkey's butt for Earth's past and history and traditions—well, enough is enough. Besides, we're the last of the Basques. The rest have long moved elsewhere. We refused to move to Paradise. What with all those genetic mutants living there. New Terra's a fresh start."

"Isn't the sparse population also an inducement?" Raven asked.

"*Sí*. We want to establish a new Basque enclave.

Like our ancestors did on Earth. Are we still expecting a two-hour trip?"

"Aye, sir," Faith said. "We'll be departing Paris Spaceport as soon as we load your cattle and possessions. We'll do a final weight check. If all's okay, we'll lift off."

"What happens if we're too heavy? Will we crash?"

"Hardly. No, we'd get an assist. They'd bring in another cruiser with the new Third Invader saucer tech. Magnetic forces. Help get us airborne if needed. We're not carrying much fuel for the hyperspace engines, nor for the sub-light ion engines. That allows us to carry more cargo. This is a quick trip. There and back again."

"Right. Then you get your maintenance done if I follow Herr Stroebel."

"Yes, a total retrofit. Our armaments are out of date. We'll get a full crew and marines too. Back to a ship-of-the-line cruiser once more. Commander Bloom can't wait for that."

"Then you'll battle the Imperium ships, eh?"

"That's the plan. No one knows for sure what the devil is going on. Why can't they be satisfied with their half the galaxy? Our side, the Federation of Planets, doesn't need to go after their half. We're still finding countless habitable planets here," Faith said.

***

After dropping him off at his cabin and Raven at hers, Faith headed to the cargo hold to inspect the situation with her own eyes.

"God, the stench," she said to the Chief of Security, whose wife walked up to them and saluted her.

She said, "XO, Captain. All secured. Doors locked and checked, ready for takeoff."

"Excellent," Faith said. "Go to your quarters and relax." She pressed the intercom button. "Sir, all secured. Ready for departure checks. To the bridge now."

Faith raced along the corridors to her bridge position in time to hear the liftoff weight check report.

"Excellent. Okay, let's get this done," Commander Bloom said. "Navigator Warden, clear our takeoff and request a liftoff assist. Pilot Trundel, get us on our way. I've already filed our flight path. Execute."

Over the ship's intercom, Commander Bloom said, "Attention. We are lifting off now. Please remain in your cabins."

The ship vibrated, but the soundproofing drowned the roaring engines, aided by the magnetic thrust from the Third Invader saucer tech, now incorporated into newer Sol Space Fleet ships. On the monitor, they watched the saucer-shaped ship aid their take off.

Five minutes later, Navigator Warden said, "Activating hyperspace engines."

Commander Bloom announced, "Entering hyperspace."

Everyone felt the stomach lurch that accompanied a ship dropping into the total blackness of hyperspace, which made travel to even the closest star possible.

Navigator Warden said, "Sir, one hour forty-six minutes to New Terra."

After announcing travel time to those onboard and turning off the intercom, Commander Bloom said, "God, the stench! We'll never get that out of here. XO, make a note we want this entire ship sterilized!"

Faith doubted sterilization would rid the ship of the foul odors, but said nothing. Ace winked at her, and she leaned back in her seat beside the Commander and dozed, dreaming of strolling Paris streets for a week until a bang and a horrid metal-ripping sound preceded a violent jerk that almost knocked her out of her seat. Sirens blared. Several unseated crew flew across the bridge, crashing into things.

Chapter 2 Aftermath

"Damage report!" Commander Bloom barked.

Pilot Ace yelled, "Hyperspace engines off line."

Navigator Warden barked, "But we're still moving through hyperspace. God knows where. Might be slowing down."

Commander Bloom ordered, "Lieutenant, fire off a distress message to Space Command. Give them our current position."

"Sir," she said, "The LDC is out. No long-distance communications."

"Stay calm, everyone. Security, check out the engine rooms. Engineer, get our hyperspace engines back online."

The two raced off.

To his XO, he said, "This is why you never, ever fly with a skeleton crew. Come on. Damage reports."

"I'll go check on the communications array," Faith said, also running as fast as possible.

"Still in hyperspace," Navigator Warden said. "I think."

"Well, either we are or aren't!"

"If we are slowing, it's barely perceptible," he said. "The readout numbers change faster than I can read them."

He took a deep breath and pressed the intercom button. "This is Commander Bloom. We have collided with something in hyperspace. Do not panic. We're still in hyperspace. This should only cause a slight delay in our arrival time. Thank you."

He turned it off.

To Ace, he said, "Can't have our passengers panicking."

Engineer Hans Bectold called in. "Sir, the hyperspace engines—they're gone. Ripped off. Our fuel is flooding into space. Wait. No, the hyperspace engine tanks are empty."

"What do you mean, gone?"

"Like something ripped that section away. Thank the gods the bulkhead doors shut or we would have all been blown out into space."

"Understood. Go check on communications and the XO. Find out why our LDC is down. We must send word to Space Command. Are we still in hyperspace?"

"Yeah, flying along. To who knows where. We're far beyond our destination, if these coordinate readouts are accurate. But if the engines are gone, sir, the readings are useless."

Their astronomer, Julie Swarmstead, said, "Sir, if we don't get out of hyperspace, we risk traveling far beyond our own galaxy. Maybe into another galaxy."

"With no engines, how can we even stop or change directions?" Navigator Warden asked.

Commander Bloom ran his hands over his head. "Okay, wild idea, Ace. Can you use the ion engines to turn our rear in the direction we're traveling? Then fire them up. That might act as a break. She's right. We could find ourselves out in intergalactic space with no hope of returning."

"On it," Ace said.

Over the intercom, Faith reported in. "Sir, the long-distance communications array is gone, along with the entire communication lab. I think the collision ripped it off, too. We'll check other areas of the ship for damage before we return."

He ran his hands through his hair again. "Okay. No hyperspace engines. No LDC. No way to call for help. Are we slowing down any?"

"Aye, sir," Navigator Warden said. "It's working. Estimate ten minutes until we drop out of hyperspace."

"Finally, we get a break. Engineer Bectold, can we build a new LDC set?"

Hans Bectold walked back onto the bridge, his face drawn and pale. "We could if the comm lab was still onboard. It held our backup systems. All of them. I can't even build one from what scraps I can find on the ship. Maybe one of our passengers brought a portable LDC with them."

"God! Why us? What else could go wrong?"

"Sir," Navigator Warden said minutes later, "we're dropping out of hyperspace now."

The familiar stomach lurch backed him up.

"Okay, on screen. Where are we? Astronomer Swarmstead, do your thing. Give us some good news. Please. Are you sure we're out of hyperspace? The screen is black."

"No, there are fuzzy spots out there. Ace, roll us over," Julie said.

Ace complied.

"Oh, shit!" Julie said.

Commander Bloom growled.

"Sir, the galaxy is behind us, assuming it's our galaxy. We're at its edge. Ace, rotate us back."

She activated her telescope. "Ah, yes, that's M31, and there's M51. Verified. Our galaxy is behind us, sir. But where are we exactly? No idea. I don't recognize any of these stars. Could use some help, sir."

"How far can we go on our ion engines, Ace, Warden?"

"Sub-light? Not far at all, sir. We'll get on the calculations now," Bill Warden said. "Come on, Ace. Let's hit the drawing board."

"Sir, what about our passengers?" XO Faith asked.

"Yeah, I know. Guess it's time to tell them we're super-fucked. Best summon the liaisons up here and face the music."

He turned the intercom to ship-wide mode.

"Attention. This is Commander Bloom. While we were in hyperspace, we collided with something that ripped off our hyperspace engines and destroyed our long-distance communications systems. It also ripped away the communication lab, so we have no way to alert Space Command of our plight. The ship continued flying through hyperspace on its own. We have brought the ship to a halt out of hyperspace.

"The bad news is that we believe we're now at the edge of our galaxy. Position: unknown. My astronomer is attempting to locate us, but if there are any astronomers among your people, have them come lend a hand. We need to know our exact location. In the meantime, will the five liaisons join me on the bridge? We can discuss our situation in depth. Thank you."

Within minutes, six passengers rushed to the bridge, Herr Stroebel leading the way.

"What the hell's going on?" he said. "Who's the idiot who ran us into something?"

Commander Bloom recognized five of them, but focused on the sixth. He, too, carried a German heritage.

"I'm Adrian Reiner, astronomer. Can I help?"

"Ah, yes, yes. The Hawker's astronomer, Lieutenant Julie Swarmstead. Give her a hand. We need to know where we are."

To the others, he explained. "Look, the engines and LDC are gone. It's a miracle we aren't corpses floating in hyperspace. Plus, the ship continued its path. Our quick thinking got us slowed and out of hyperspace. Our first guess is we're somewhere at the edge of the galaxy. I need the astronomers to pinpoint our location. You need to keep your people calm while we work this out."

"How in infernal hell can you work this out, Commander?" Herr Stroebel said, his face reddening. "I demand you get us to New Terra as planned."

XO Koralsky said, "Look. Here's the situation. All we have right now is ion sub-light engines. If we were on Earth and using them, the absolute fastest we could get to the nearest star, Proxima Centauri, is four years. We have neither food nor water for such a lengthy journey. Besides, with all the animals onboard, what would they eat? We need calm, rational ideas right now. For example, if we could land somewhere, there's a chance we could repair the damage and be on our way."

"Good God! We're stranded in nowhere, with no

chance of returning to civilization or summoning help. We're all going to die out here because of some fool's error," Herr Stroebel said.

Commander Bloom nodded. XO Koralsky grimaced and spoke up.

"We're not dead yet. There are a multitude of bright people on this ship," she said. "We're trying to find our precise position and examine options."

"Right," Raven said. "If we can find a habitable place to land, perhaps with everyone working together, we can repair the ship."

"Hopeful drivel," the German said and stomped off the bridge.

"Are you guys making any progress on the ship's position?" Raven asked, changing the depressed mood on the bridge.

Adrian said, "Well, maybe. Julie located a G class star like Earth's sun. It's the biggest and nearest star. Right now, we can't find it in the star catalogs."

"Don't most such stars have planets?" Faith asked.

Julie said, "Yes, most do. But this one has a red dwarf companion. It's a double star. We're searching for planets around the G star. So far, nada."

"Keep looking," the XO said. "I don't think we've enough sub-light ion engine fuel or survival means to travel much beyond this system."

"Precisely," the navigator said.

Adrian said, "Julie and I think we're looking at the Outer Arm, which lies beyond the Perseus Arm. Sol lies in the Orion Spur arm, just inside the Perseus Arm. If that helps."

"We're in trouble for sure," Warden said. "The Federation hasn't explored the Perseus Arm, let alone the Outer Arm. Too remote. Cass-C, seat of the Federation, is close to the central bar in the Norma Arm. We really *are* on our own."

Julie said, "No luck yet. The red dwarf star has perturbed any planets around the G star out of the solar system. Going to try the dwarf next, but not much hope with it."

"It produces massive amounts of infrared radiation. We studied those in a physics class," Raven said. "Any habitable planet around one of those would be tucked in close to it. I had to do a habitable zone calculation once in Light Class."

"That's where we're looking now," Adrian said.

Engineer Hans Bectold reported in from airlock one. "Permission to go EVA, Commander. I'm streaming video now. You'll see what I'm seeing—and help me assess the damage in real time."

"Permission granted for EVA. For god's sake, Hans, be careful. We've only got one more spacesuit. Damn this whole damn venture. I should never have agreed to it."

"We needed the retrofit," Faith said.

"And now that's likely pointless," he said, running his hands over his head again.

Total silence fell on the bridge. All eyes stared at the video being streamed up on a large monitor showing what Hans saw as he made his careful way down the outer side of the cigar-shaped silver ship.

For the benefit of the liaisons, Faith said, "He's wearing magnetic boots. And he's fastened to a safety line. But an EVA is always a risky move."

"Holy shit! You guys seeing this?" Hans said, leaning over so his head camera got a better view of the gaping hole where the hyperspace engines used to be. A huge gouge or rip in the skin appeared where the communications lab had been. "Glancing blow. Probably saved our lives."

"Good work, Hans. Head back. Nothing you can do out there," the commander said. He turned to his XO. "We're dead men standing."

"Don't give up, Commander," Faith said. "We land and make repairs."

"I need a drink. Hopeless. I've a date with my fifty-year-old Beam. You have the bridge, XO."

Commander Bloom ambled out of the room, heading for his quarters and the bottle of old whiskey he'd been saving.

"He's taking this hard, isn't he?" Raven whispered to Faith, who nodded and joined the astronomers.

The other liaisons returned to their groups, but Zigor came back.

"XO, the sedation is wearing off the animals. We don't have enough to re-sedate them. Rafael says their horses are getting skiddy, too. Thought you ought to know." He left.

A tense, but silent, half hour passed before Julie brightened up. "Guys, I've found a habitable planet. It's around the red dwarf. Adrian and I are calculating its orbit. We believe it has a breathable atmosphere."

Faith said, "Bill, plot a course to this planet. Ace, take us there without riling up the animals."

Ace laughed. "XO, I don't know how to rile up animals. But I'll fly us as smoothly as possible."

Grinning, Faith said, "Make it so, Ace. I'll make a ship-wide announcement. We don't want panic when the passengers feel the acceleration. Do we have enough fuel?"

"For sure. It's quite close to us," Bill Warden said.

"Attention everyone. This is XO Koralsky. We've located what we believe is a habitable planet around the red dwarf star. We're flying there now. I'll give you an ETA as soon as I can. With some luck, we can land, repair the damage, and resume our trip. That's all for now."

Chapter 3 Land Fall

"What do we know about this planet? Good news, please," Commander Bloom said, slurring slightly. The smell of his aged Beam permeated the bridge.

"We're still working out the details, sir," Julie said. "It orbits the red dwarf. Adrian is timing its rotation while Raven and I calculate its orbital period. It's darn close to its dwarf sun, though. As we get closer, we'll be able to tell you more. Initial look is promising, sir."

"A day is about twenty hours long, sir," Adrian said. "Four more revolutions and I'll have it down to the minutes."

"Excellent. Twenty hours works for me," Commander Bloom said.

"We've an initial guess on revolutions," Julie said. "It revolves around the red dwarf in about twenty of its days. We'll need more observations to tell how long it and the red dwarf take to orbit the G-type star. It's in an elliptical orbit. Raven's doing those calculations now."

Raven said, "Looks like perihelion is about Earth's distance from Sol or 1 AU. But aphelion is about Mars' distance from the sun. Expect extreme variations in G star's heating of this world."

"Telling the daytime hours will be tricky," Julie said. "When the red sun rises, the yellow sun might have set or already risen or even just rising, too. Expect a complex relationship between daylight and its heating effects."

"Boggles my mind," Faith said. "We're setting up the IR camera now. And the spectrometer."

The Commander scrunched up his face, so Raven said, "That'll give us some idea of the surface temperature and the atmospheric composition. Just hope the air is breathable."

Navigator Warden said, "We should achieve orbit

above the planet by eight tomorrow morning."

"Good. Good. I'll turn in. You still have the bridge, XO."

Commander Bloom stumbled from the room.

"Did you smell the alcohol?" Julie whispered to Faith, who nodded.

"With this skeleton crew, none of us will get much rest until we can land," Faith said. "Who can I put in charge of the Hawker? We'll need a fresh and alert crew when we arrive."

The communications officer said, "XO, I'm not needed now. No communications to handle. Get some sleep. We could ask Dr. Marshal Wu and Nurse Vita Vega to come up and help. Just tell us what to do and you, Ace, and Bill can catch some shuteye."

"We sure as hell didn't plan on this. A skeleton crew should have been enough," Faith said, yawning. "Thanks. Let's do that. We can't afford a botched landing because Ace and Bill are sleep deprived. The animal stench has already breached the bridge."

"Good, we caught you in time!" Jessica said, as she and Sam, the Chiefs of Security, rushed onto the bridge.

"We've figured out why the collision happened," Sam said. "We went over the data logs and found it."

"Good work. What happened?" the XO asked, as the entire bridge crew stopped work to listen.

"As you know, our deflector shield pushes smaller bits aside. The collision alert warning activates automatically when the ship runs into a more massive chunk of debris than the shield can shunt aside."

"But we got no collision warning. I swear," Ace said, rubbing his face.

"That's because none came," Jessica said. "There's a loose electrical connection in those circuits. The hyperspace jump jarred the connection."

"When the shields tried to send the collision alert, it never activated," Sam said.

"Before we go much farther, we gotta fix that loose connection or we could ram into something else," Jessica said.

“Well done, both of you. I’ll get Hans on it immediately,” Faith said, activating the intercom. “Engineer, to the bridge ASAP.”

Ace said, “I’ll take the helm and monitor the radar. Since we’re not in hyperspace, we should have plenty of warning next time.”

***

Early the next morning, Raven joined the other liaisons on the bridge but smelled alcohol on the commander’s breath. *He looks a bit ragged.*

Commander Bloom addressed the bridge crew. His XO had briefed him on last night’s discoveries, and he had the five liaisons witness today’s events, for good or for ill. He explained the reason for the collision, and that Hans had repaired the loose connection.

He slurred, “Ahead is the planet we hope to land on and make repairs. I’ll let our astronomer fill you in on the details. Julie...”

“Yes. It has a mass close to Earth’s. A good sign. It’s within the habitable zone of the red dwarf star, which is in an elliptical orbit around the G-type star, resulting in bizarre variables on the planet. It’s easier to understand in terms of local variables. The length of the planet’s day is twenty hours, using our measurement of hours. The planet is quite close to the red dwarf, so its orbital period, which on Earth would be the length of its year, is twenty of the planet’s days. The planet is speeding around the red dwarf. But the red dwarf itself orbits the G-type star, which is comparable to our Sol. We’ll need far more observation to determine that orbit’s complete properties. But initially we believe its perihelion distance is about 1 AU, like Earth, while at aphelion, it’s 1.5 AU, like Mars.

“The planet’s position with respect to the G star determines this planet’s seasons, unlike Earth. Right now, our belief is that it’s likely spring. Adrian has been making detailed observations.”

“Yes,” Adrian said, “it’s habitable. It has oceans of water. Its atmosphere has a slightly higher oxygen content than Earth. Nitrogen levels are parallel to Earth. Phosphorous content is much higher than Earth, but tolerable. Surface temperature varies, based on whether the red dwarf is overhead and/or the G star. It's a confusing mess. Best I can say so far is that winters will be quite cold, while the summers won't be brutally hot. We can land on this world and deal with repairs."

Ace spoke next. "We're in planet viewing range now. We've not detected lights in the night sky or radio waves. Nothing suggests a modern civilization. Who knows what we'll find? I'm taking us into a high orbit. Our first view of the planet is on the video screens."

"All I see is water." Commander Bloom grumbled.

"We're landing on water? What kind of fools are you people?" Herr Stroebel barked.

"Looks like the Pacific Ocean," XO Koralsky said. "Remember, Earth is 70% water."

"Is that a mountain ahead?" Raven asked. *That should satisfy Stroebel.* She smiled at and nodded to Faith, who nodded back.

"We're moving from east to west," Ace said. "This mountain range marks the eastern edge of the continent."

"You can't land in mountains, can you?" Herr Stroebel asked, curling up his mouth.

"Ah, look. Rolling hills," Faith said.

"And green," Raven added. *Stroebel should keep his mouth shut!*

"Make that dark green. It's an extensive, rather dark forest," Adrian said. "Is that a wide river we're following?"

"Sure looks like it," Ace said.

"You can't land in a forest, dummkopfs!" Herr Stroebel said.

Raven bit her lip to stifle her urge to tell him to shut up.

A bit later, extensive grasslands appeared. White-capped mountains marked the northern boundary of the continent, which yielded to another dark forest land. A small set of mountains appeared through which two rivers merged and flowed south. Further south, they glimpsed another east-west river that joined the larger one flowing south. Huge grasslands with trees interspersed covered this section of the continent.

Rolling hills lined the western edge of the continent before the blue appeared again. On the next pass, Ace brought them further south. Here, the mountains gave way to a reddish desert region at the extreme southeastern edge of the continent before yielding to flat grassland. Close to where that large river flowed south to the ocean, three small peaks rose. The river ended in a southern swampy delta. Across the broad river, the rolling hills continued to the western shore as before.

Later passes uncovered no other continents. A lower pass showed no signs of human-level intelligence habitations, though it didn't rule out hamlets or rural villages.

"Okay, Ace, let's land in the grasslands near those three small peaks. It's probably warmer this far south, and the water is close," Commander Bloom said. He activated the intercom and made the announcement.

Zigor said, "The sedation has long worn off the animals. Be careful, please."

The XO said, "Ace, make like you're landing on a pile of eggshells!"

First, Ace maneuvered the heavy cruiser lower and closer to the trio of small, rocky peaks. As they did so, the ship spooked a herd of antlered animals, grazing on the spring grasses. Winds rocked the ship and caused animal fearful cries heard throughout the ship.

"Well, there's animal life," Zigor said. "That's encouraging. What'll we call them?"

Raven said, "They look sort of like caribou. Let's call them that. Caribou. I know they aren't the same, but we're likely to see many things that are similar. Using Earth terms is much simpler than inventing names, since we don't have botanists and zoologists with us."

Zigor laughed. "I like your thinking, Miss Cooper. Caribou they are. I wonder if they are friendly."

"This is getting tricky," Ace said. "We're overloaded.

Without a magnetic assist, this could be a rough landing."

"Do the best you can," Commander Bloom said. "Just don't damage the Hawker any further."

Raven held her breath. Others on the bridge did as well. She crossed her fingers, as did Faith. The two noticed each other and nodded.

The ground grew larger. Ace slowed their descent. With the ship lurching, he fought the controls to achieve a wobbling hover a few feet above the ground before a thud announced landfall. Ace shut down the ion engines.

"Very well done, Ace. Good landing under the circumstances," Commander Bloom said. To the liaisons, he said, "We can't just charge outside. We need air quality tests. There could be millions of plants and animals out there that might kill us. Where is a fully equipped deep space exploration ship when you need it? Liaisons, go back to your constituents and see what you have available for plant and animal identification, either the machines or scientists. We need to know what's safe and what isn't ASAP. I want the animals off my ship soon, but not if something out there is deadly to them. We have very little such equipment onboard. Our security team will exit first, testing as they go."

"But the animals need to eat and drink soon," Zigor said.

"True, but we don't know what dangers this planet holds for us. Use extreme caution."

The liaisons returned to their people.

***

Faith and Commander Bloom watched the EVA of the Chief of Security, Captain Sam Smeltzer. He wore a full spacesuit. Using a handheld air sampler, he tested the air, pointing his head camera onto the device readout. He took temperature readings.

"Removing helmet now."

They watched as he laid it aside.

"The air smells fresh and clean. Bit of an odor, though. Temperature is fifty-five, tad chilly. Ah, the red sun is heating my face. Testing more now."

He passed a wand over the grass, detecting moisture as well, before collecting a bit of dirt beneath the grass.

"So far, all clear. Coming in now. Get a repair crew out here."

Chapter 4 First Steps

"Looks like the hand of God ripped off that entire section of the ship. It's a miracle we weren't all killed," Raven said to XO Koralsky, as she and the Hawker crew surveyed the Hawker's damage. She cinched the hood on her jacket tighter, leaving nothing visible except her eyes. *Should have brought my winter coat.*

"Bulkheads are strong and meant to take serious damage," Faith said. "That section there is where the engines were. Just ripped away. Whatever destroyed the communication lab continued through to the engines. The deflector shields did what they're supposed to. If the collision warning had worked, Ace could have avoided the damage."

"If, if, if. Now what do we do? Is this repairable?" she asked.

The XO sighed. "Between us, I don't know how, but the Commander insists it is repairable. Maybe he has an ace up his sleeve. If so, that's why I'm only an XO."

Raven's eyes scanned the grasslands. *I agree. No way they can repair all that out here in the middle of nowhere.* "If we could get a message back to—" She shrugged her shoulders. "Won't someone miss us and send a rescue ship?"

Faith shook her head. "Look, ships are always running into hidden or black objects. Flying around space is dangerous. We all know the risks. On average, Space Force loses a ship each year. They can trace the Hawker up to its hyperspace entry, right after liftoff in Paris. After that, they're clueless. Sure, they'll send a search crew to New Terra and then mark us as lost in space. Another space industry casualty."

Then, we really are screwed. Stranded. Make the best of it, Raven.

The XO said, "That's why the LDC, the long-distance communication device, is revolutionary. An ordinary comm system signal from Proxima Centauri to Earth takes four years to get there. The LDC sends through hyperspace from Proxima Centauri to Earth taking a minute or less. The invention of the LDC is one of the most vital advances ever, tied only with the invention of the hyperspace engine."

"Can you guys build a new one?" Raven asked. "An LDC?"

"In that lab there. The one that's totally gone. We're hoping one of you settlers brought one along."

"Since they told us New Terra had lots of LDC sets and since weight was a premium, that's doubtful," Raven said. *We're stuck here. God!*

"Once we get the animals off-loaded, Commander Bloom will have us scour every nook and cranny of the ship looking for anything we can use to build an LDC or make new engines. Forget the engines; we lost all its fuel as well, so a new engine is useless. No, I'm hoping for an LDC."

"Otherwise, we're stranded here?" Raven asked, voicing her conclusion aloud and looking for confirmation.

XO Koralsky nodded. "But please, not a word about that just yet. We don't want a panic. Give the Commander a chance."

Raven walked over to where Zigor and his group dealt with their cows. He spotted her and waved.

"We're building electric-fenced pastures, like we planned to do on New Terra. It'll keep the cows separated from the bulls and the milk cows in a field of their own."

"Looks like they like the grass—kind of like Earth grass, but I'm not a plant person," she said.

"Aye, it's different, but the cows seem to like it. We're bringing a UTV out now. We'll use it to haul water from the river to the herd. We've tested it for purity and microbes. So far, so good. But any word on the ship? Looks pretty bad."

"Ship is still flight-worthy. Not that it matters without an engine and the long-distance communication rig. Our best hope lies in finding a working LCD and calling for rescue. Smart idea bringing that UTV along. But how much gas do you have?"

Zigor sighed. "Sí. A rescue would be ideal. Not enough gas, if we're stuck here. Ah, here comes Rafael with their horses."

"Their fencing is taller than yours."

Zigor laughed. "Cows don't jump. Much. The Scotts have herding dogs, so they don't need fences. You know what's curious? Those caribou. Look at them sniffing around the cow and horse pens. I hope there are no big predators around."

"Or bugs and viruses," Raven added.

"Or parasites that make our horses ill. We have limited vet supplies," Rafael said, joining the two and watching the unfolding scene.

"Isn't it amazing that way out here on the very edge of the galaxy we find plants and animals have developed?" Zigor said.

Koralsky, overhearing them, said, "Yes, nearly everywhere we go, we find evidence of some forms of life. Makes one wonder if there is a god somewhere that's made all this possible. Perhaps some of the invader races had something to do with it. We fought off the Sixth Invaders on Earth. And we've had many interactions with the Third Invaders, adopting their magnetic propulsion tech. But we know so little about the other invaders."

"Perhaps," Rafael said, "its only has to do with the right chemical stew as planets evolve. Micro-organisms can do amazing things. My son is studying those found in the underwater abysses of Earth's oceans. Who can say? Say, what are the chances of us getting rescued?"

Faith shrugged her shoulders and sighed. "Given that the hyperspace engines are totally gone, everything depends on acquiring a working LDC."

"How far can the ship get on its ion engines?" Zigor asked.

"At sub-light speeds, you don't want to know. The next nearest star, according to Julie, is ten light years distant. The bare minimum would be ten years, but we can't go anywhere near as fast as light. More like twenty years. But we lack fuel for that distance, let alone food and water, even if we abandoned all the animals. No, a working LDC is our best chance, guys."

Raven said, "Either find or make a LDC and send a message or this is our new home. We could do a lot worse than this planet." *Best to plant the right idea.*

Many others wandered out, eager to see this world, breathe fresh air, and get away from the overpowering stench the animals had made. Raven heard the Stroebel teens before they and their Dad joined the small group around the XO.

Hanna said, "Dad! How could you bring us here? No phone service. No houses. No shops. No stores. No nothing. This is beyond shitty."

"Yeah, Dad. Take us home—like now. Make it happen like you're always telling us."

Herr Stroebel ignored their whining. "Air smells funny, but what a relief from the manure-flooded ship. Can't we air it out? And how are the repairs coming along? Rafael. Zigor. Raven."

"Hey, demand she take us home, like *now*!" Hanna said, making no attempt to keep Faith from hearing her.

While Herr Stroebel ignored her outburst, Raven didn't.

"See that?" Raven pointed to the rear of the ship. "See the hyperspace engines? Right. They're not there. No engines. See that gaping hole? No long-distance communications either. Ion engines go sub-light only. In case you don't know what that is, top speed might be ninety thousand miles a second. To get to the nearest star from here would take the ship about eight years. To get home, if we even knew what direction to go, would take about twenty thousand years. Don't think you'll live that long. So grow up."

"Oh, I see you don't have any children yet. In time, you'll learn to ignore the kids, Miss Cooper," Herr Stroebel said. "So, XO Koralsky, has your engineers made any progress on building new engines or a new LDC set? I'm sure they'll send a rescue ship just as soon as word reaches them of *my* plight."

Rafael said, "I've had my people look through everything we brought with us for anything that could be used as an LDC. Nothing so far. We thought bringing more horses would be better than bringing along supposedly unneeded equipment. Ah, here come the chickens."

All eyes turned to watch Dusty Baker leading her group out of the cargo hold, carrying chicken crates. She called out as she walked over to them.

"Anyone for fresh eggs?"

Raven smiled. *What I would give for real scrambled eggs right now.*

"Don't worry. We left them in your galley. Your cook is using them for supper. Is it safe to let the birds out of their cages? Any predators seen?"

Faith said, "As long as they don't take off. We've seen caribou-like animals. No predators yet. There are insects and the occasional birds about. If we had a normal deep space exploration crew, we could survey the planet and identify plants and animals properly. Since we don't. What you see," she swept her arms across the wide panorama, "is what we see. I just hope there aren't spiders or mosquitoes. Can't stand either."

Dusty laughed. "Spiders give me the creeps! Can't avoid them on a chicken farm, though. They love a barnyard. Okay, we'll gamble with a few for now. Trouble is, we didn't bring along much feed for them. Soon, they'll need forage. We'll know what's in the soil soon enough. The chickens will scratch up anything that moves."

"Best keep them some distance from the electric fences," Rafael said.

Dog barking broke the stillness, followed by a tidal wave of gray wooly sheep as hundreds of sheep and a few goats clamored out of the ship. While the first ones out wanted to stop and devour the lush grasses, the border collies continued to bark and urge them on towards a couple shepherds walking way out beyond the electric fences and the chicken crates.

Bain Macnab, his wife, and kids strolled over to the group.

"Air smells refreshing. Was getting rather stuffy in there. Hi, XO Koralsky. Bet your ship wasn't designed to handle that volume of odors."

She smiled. "Right on that. We calculated it would be okay for the two-hour trip, except..."

"Right. Jesus, that's one gigantic hole in the ship! A miracle we're still alive."

"Aye. The bulkheads are designed to take such punishment. After all, the Hawker is a heavy cruiser, built for space battles. But losing the engines..."

"Makes sense. So, is that where the communications laboratory was located?"

"Aye, sir."

"Kids, look at what that space collision did to the ship. Impressive technology to take such a massive hit and keep flying."

"But Dad, no engines. How are we going to get home?" his son asked. "Or anywhere?"

"Leave that up to Commander Bloom. That's his job. Right?"

"Aye, but it's all of our crew's job," Faith corrected him. "Since you're all off the ship, I'll lend them a hand. Wow! Look at that!"

She pointed to the eastern sky where the red sun had just risen.

"Gosh, that's a gigantic sun!" the boy said.

Raven said, "That's because this planet orbits very close to it. The G-type sun overhead is like our Sol and right now is farther away from here than the Earth is from Sol, so it appears so much smaller. But yes, that red dwarf sun sure is freaky looking. Wow! Now you can feel its heat."

"Why is that?" the boy asked.

"Most of the red dwarf's radiation is in the infrared. Only a little bit comes out in the optical range, very unlike the G sun," Raven said. "Hence, this red sun provides mostly infrared heat to this world. To make this a habitable world, it must orbit the red sun very close to it, like Mercury does with Sol. Hey, I bet this world will have some amazing eclipses of the yellow sun by the red sun."

"I'd rather go home or to this new world my folks promised us."

"Well, like yeah," Hanna spoke up. "That's what I keep telling Dad. We want to go home. This place sucks. No phone service. No stores. No people. No nothing."

"We can text others on the ship," his daughter said. "But that's not the same. Is it? Have you guys got any of the latest games on your phone? Like Crazy Aces? Dad says it's too violent for us."

Hanna and the kids moved away from the adults, whispering to each other. Raven glimpsed Hanna's phone screen and saw the game's splash screen.

"They are on an exciting new world full of things never seen before," Raven said, "and they are only interested in their phones. Kids!"

"Like I said," Herr Stroebel said, "it's best to ignore them. Have any of your people got an LDC set or the parts needed to build one? Somehow, I must get off this world and back to civilization."

Sometimes it's best to ignore the adults, Raven thought.

Chapter 5 Reality Wins

The next day, XO Faith Koralsky made her usual rounds, thanking security for their herculean efforts to clean the cargo hold and air out the stench. Then she checked with the astronomers, thankful the German had continued to assist the Hawker's astronomer. The young woman, like the engineer, shouldered an impossible load going forward.

"By some triangulation methods using the galaxies and nebula we can see," she said, "we are still in the Milky Way galaxy and in our half, removing the threat of attack by Imperium cruisers claiming we're invading their half. Trouble is, XO, we can't identify a single star. If we had an LDC, we wouldn't know which direction to point its antenna. Somewhere that'a way isn't good enough."

"It's not her fault, XO," the German said. "The Federation hasn't star mapped the outer arm. We're attempting an impossible task. Today, we'll search for O and A-type stars, along with super giants, in hopes we can make a positive ID of one of those super-luminous stars. If we can locate two, we can fix our position a hundred times more accurately."

"Excellent work under impossible conditions. Best of luck today. Carry on."

Both flashed a smile as she headed down to the engineering lab where most of the crew had gathered.

"Hans, morning report," Faith said.

"Not good. There are no LDC sets onboard. The parts needed to build a new one were in the communication lab. I've got one guy researching processes to make the fuel we'd need and another working out how to build an engine from scratch. Not much chance of success, though. Everyone else is studying the schematics of the ship for parts to build a new LDC set. We can make the antenna easily enough. Permission to cannibalize the ship's systems."

"Everything but life support. We'll turn to that as a last resort. But yes, tear this ship apart to find a way to send a distress call. Keep me posted."

"Will do. Commander's taking this hard. He got drunk last night. We haven't bothered him today."

Faith smiled. "Understood. He's my responsibility. Carry on. Keep me posted."

Next, she dropped by sickbay and found Dr. Marshal Wu holding a conference with five other doctors from the various groups.

"Morning, XO," Dr. Wu said. "Join us. We're going over our findings from yesterday."'

"Excellent. What's the latest?"

"Tests show no parasites or microbes incompatible with human bodies in the river water. Tiny traces of urine, likely from the caribou and other animals. The water is remarkably clean, compared to what we're used to seeing on Earth. The vets agree the grasses are okay for the animals to graze, as if we could prevent them from grazing."

Several chuckles punctuated the air.

"The key question is which of the flora and fauna are harmful to humans. And I'm afraid that'll require trial and error. Trouble is, we're doctors, not scientists. We will poll the others in our respective groups and see if we can get help there. Oh, please thank Dusty Baker for the eggs. That omelet last night hit the spot."

"Excellent. Keep me posted."

Faith headed outside, where the hundreds of others gathered. One member of the German group held the group's attention.

"Right. I talked with a crew member last night. It's doable. They've got five shuttles we could borrow. Why don't we explore five regions? We'll take the mountain ranges to the east. Bain, I know those far northern rolling hills appeal to your people."

"And the hills to the west might make excellent horse breeding lands," Rafael said. "We'll go that way."

Zigor said, "We'll go south. Who wants the dark forests to the north?"

"We do," a member of the English group said. "We're curious about the lakes and trees there."

"Everyone, stay alert. Lord knows what's out there. Take no chances. Commander Bloom will have our hides if we damage one of his shuttles. Er, I assume we can use them, XO Koralsky. Didn't see you arriving."

"Sure. I'll help you get them out of the landing bay. I assume you have qualified pilots," Faith said. *If we're stuck here, those five craft become our most valuable asset.*

"Thanks. Any progress to report?" one asked.

"Not yet. We're looking for the materials to build a new LDC set. The astronomers are slowly zeroing in on our position. May know more tonight."

Later, Faith watched, as the shuttles lifted into the sky and headed off on exploration runs. She sighed and headed to the commander's quarters to make her morning report, wondering if it mattered anymore. She found him still drunk, but gave her report anyway.

"Ya think Hans can find enough parts in the ship to make a new LDC?" he asked. "I sure as hell don't. We're stuck here. We're all gonna die. Ya know what's worse, Koralsky? We're gonna miss the big war. Finally, we get to fight actual battles, an' we're stuck here. That's the shits!" He took another long swill from an almost empty whisky bottle.

"We must have faith in our engineers."

"Piss in one hand and pour faith in the other. See which one fills up first. Even if some miracle happens and Hans makes a new hyperspace engine, we got no fuel for it. And we both know there are no components for a new LDC set anywhere else on the ship. No, Koralsky, we're stuck here until we die."

She didn't bother responding and left. *He's drunk. Can't say I blame him. He's being honest with me. We got no engines and no way to make new ones. I couldn't build a LDC set if my life depended on it. What the hell can we do if we're stuck here? Gods, Faith, snap out of it. Get your head up. Keeping morale up is on you now. Encourage your crew. They'll find a way out of this mess.*

Her Communications Officer requested her help in the galley. *It's gotta be a food issue.*

"Morning Sally. So sorry we forced you into chief cook."

The short-haired blond young woman said, "It's not your fault. We didn't bring Chef Rollie. No one knew we'd be in this kind of trouble. Just a two-hour flight. Well, as you know, I've had our guests coming by in shifts of a hundred at a time. Dusty Baker's daily donation of eggs is the only thing I've got left for food. I've used up our stock, except the emergency blue goo rations and the K-rations. By lunchtime, people are going to be hungry. What do you want me to do?"

"How long will the K-rations last for us?"

"Just a guess, but maybe two weeks at the most."

"Okay. Use them. Make up a sign that explains the mush contains a balanced diet but tastes like crap. Er, best say that better."

Both women chuckled.

"Pilots, scour this world for food sources." She activated the intercom. "This is XO Koralsky. Will the five liaisons please report to the galley? Thanks."

"I'll put on a new pot of coffee. At least we have lots of that," Sally said.

One by one, the others joined her.

Over coffee, Faith explained. "We've run out of food. We didn't come prepared to feed thousands. We still have emergency blue goo; it's awful, but can sustain life. Before we go there, we have canned K-rations, which taste—well, you'll find out. Sally estimates we can get by on those for two weeks."

"How soon do we expect rescue?" Herr Stroebel asked, his face twisted in a snarl.

"Unknown, sir. We've made some progress on ascertaining our location, but so far we've found nothing we can use to make a new LDC set. Of course, without engines, the ship isn't going anywhere. We must tighten our belts and get by until we can make a new LDC set and get word to Space Force."

Raven asked, "So what can we do to help with the food situation?"

"First, does your group have any food you can donate?" Silence and shaking heads.

"It was only supposed to be a couple of hours," Herr Stroebel said, "and now we're all doomed to starvation on this godforsaken wasteland. All thanks to your incompetence."

Raven said, "Hold on. You can't blame XO Koralsky. Space collisions happen frequently. I'm told we lose one ship a year. And their engineer explained how the accident happened. We need positive suggestions."

"Thanks, Miss Cooper," Faith said. "That's why I asked you here. Today, I'd like your groups fanning out across this world on a hunter-gatherer type mission. See if you can find anything edible. Preferably, that won't kill or make us sick."

Raven laughed. After a moment, the others joined her. Except Herr Stroebel.

The XO said, "On each shuttle is a poison detector device. You can use it to test potential food sources. Unlike the cows, we can't eat the grass, which seems the most abundant thing around here."

Zigor said, "We will get on this right away. But has the Commander given any thought about what happens if we cannot get a rescue?"

Grunts and head nods supported his question. Until now, no one dared ask that aloud.

Koralsky ran her hands across her face, pausing before answering. "Honestly? No. None of us dare think such thoughts. Not yet. I've not given up on our engineers. Between us, our only hope is assembling a new LDC set and getting through to Space Force. Obviously, the ship will never fly again. Let's not go there just yet. Give my engineers time to work a miracle. Meantime, see if your people can find edibles on this world."

She said, "Slaughtering your animals is off the table, as their offspring is our lifeline to a future." *I see relief on their faces.* "Best of luck with your hunter-gathering today. That is all."

As they filed out, Herr Stroebel said, "We could always butcher some of your cows. I'd love a T-Bone about now."

Zigor replied. "Over my dead body!"

Koralsky watched them go. *Sure glad we locked the armory, but maybe some extra security would be wise. Best check with Hans. God, my stomach is one massive knot! Even the unspoken thought of us stuck here makes me sick.*

Bits and electronic equipment lay scattered around Hans when she found him in the engineering lab. A curl of smoke rose from his soldering iron. He looked up. His face told her all. He exhaled, and his shoulders slumped. Hans shook his head.

"No success?"

"Not unless you can find me a phylo-calculating-microchip somewhere on this ship that I've overlooked. I can make everything in a new LDC except that component. Which is the key part that sends signals through hyperspace. Without that, all I've got here is a local broadcasting unit. Using it, I'll be dead a hundred times over before Space Force gets my message. I can't. Make a new LDC. All is lost."

Hans broke down, sobbing. Faith put a comforting arm on his shoulders.

"It's not your fault, Hans. We'll survive somehow. Let's get the entire crew together and brainstorm ideas. Shall we?"

"It's no use, XO. We're doomed."

Quietly, Koralsky rounded up the two dozen crew members and closed the bridge doors. Commander Bloom sat in his chair, oblivious to the world.

Julie said, "Gang, we have verified we are in the outer arm, about here." She pointed out a dot in the spiral arms image of the Federation of Planet's half. "We're at least fifteen thousand light years from home. We can't do more than give an approximate position for any LDC signal. I recommend sending the signal at a hundred different angles. One might get through."

Hans shook his head. His blood-shot eyes spoke volumes. Koralsky saved him by speaking for him.

"Gang, try as we might, we just don't have the key part on this ship to make a new LDC set work. It's a phylo-something or other. Our distress call will take fifteen thousand years to reach Space Force. Does anyone have any bright ideas or wild ideas?"

"Bill and I have gone over all the schematics for the hyperspace engines," Pilot Ace Trundel said. "We figured if we had all the parts, we might build one. But..."

"No parts," Faith said.

Pushing himself up with his hands and using the arms of his chair to keep upright, Commander Bloom spoke, attempting to avoid slurring his words.

"My dearest crew. This is the end of our journey. We're not getting off this planet. No rescue is coming. We're out of options. At times like these, the captain's duty is to issue the 'abandon ship' order. My last action as your commander is to order you to abandon ship. You are all free from your obligation to serve the Hawker and Space Force. You may do as you will. I will make the announcement to our guests next. You have been the best crew a commander could ever have wanted. Now it's time to go."

He pressed the intercom button. His voice carried throughout the ship and outside.

"Your attention. This is Space Force Commander Silas Bloom of the heavy cruiser Hawker. We have no engines. We have no long-distance communications ability. We are fifteen thousand light years from home and stranded on this barely habitable planet without hope of rescue and no hope of survival. I've ordered my crew to abandon ship. This is the end. Make your own peace as suits you. That is all."

To the crew, he said, "Retiring to my cabin. Bless

you all."

The solemn crew watched him stagger from the bridge. Koralsky suspected in the back of their minds that the crew already knew they were stranded here forever, but the stunned silence spoke volumes. No one knew what to say or do.

"Well, shit! That's that. Okay, I don't aim to die just yet. If we work together, we can survive. Anyone with me?"

"Yeah, I am," Ace said.

"We all are," Hans said. "But what now?"

"Join forces with our guests."

Chapter 6 Marooned

As their official liaison, Raven gathered her group together to see about hunting and gathering, per Koralsky's request, when the commander's announcement came, sending shockwaves through the hundreds of immigrants. It confirmed what many had been thinking all along, but it devastated many others. After the initial shock, some shrieked protests of denial while others broke down, sobbing.

They should have guessed this, Raven thought. *When I first saw the damage, I knew the outcome. We're going to starve unless they act. I must get them onto a survival path.*

Raven looked at the group of almost five hundred men, women, and a few children and said, "Look, everyone. We're not dead yet. I think we all suspected we'd be stranded here when we first saw that happened to the ship. It's just that we've been trying to ignore that. While I looked forward to my new teaching assignment on New Terra, that's not happening. But I can still teach here. If we can survive. Look, we have the right animals and plant seeds for survival. Plenty of people. We'll make a new civilization here on Landfall. That's what I'm calling this world. Look. We either work together and somehow survive or we just give up and die. I don't want to die. Not just yet."

One woman wailed, "It's hopeless! No food. No houses. No nothing. It's an empty world. We're the walking dead."

"No medical facilities," another said. "I'm seven months pregnant. What's going to happen to me and my baby?"

"Right," her husband said. "Doctor Johnson can deliver our boy, but if anything goes even slightly wrong..."

"This is total crap!" The voice of Herr Stroebel from

the German group intruded. “We are all as good as dead. I’ve been saying that all along. Now the commander has confirmed it. There’s absolutely nothing here. We can’t survive here. It’ll be worse than the Dark Ages.”

Someone else yelled, “More like ancient hunter-gatherer nomads, assuming there’s anything to hunt or gather!”

One of the Spanish group yelled, “*Como yo lo veo*, the only question remaining is, do you want to die now or prolong it by putting it off a week or a month when the food supplies run out?”

A man from the German group said, “Look, I’d like to make a go of it, if the other groups will share their animals and feed with us. Trouble is, we don’t have any equipment. No axes to cut down trees. No shovels, plows. We lack basic tools to make homes and farms. So maybe he’s right. It’s a matter of how long do we want to prolong our inevitable deaths.”

Another man said, “And how soon before we fight each other for the last scraps of food?”

I must do something. “What if we can find local sources of food?” Raven said. “Then we won’t starve. Maybe we can cannibalize the ship to make the tools we need. Let’s do what Koralsky asked us to do today and fan out and search for food. We shouldn’t give up without a fight.”

“The ship provides shelter for now,” Koralsky said. “Life support runs off the small nuclear power pack, giving us lights, heat, and cooking facilities. That should last a long time. Years, likely. It’ll give us more time to work out details.”

Thank God, someone’s backing me up! “She’s right. We’ve got shelter with the ship. All we need right away is food,” Raven said. “Let’s take this one step at a time.”

Hanna screamed, “What about us kids? We didn’t ask to be here. There’s absolutely nothing out there. Are we supposed to be hermits in a cave or something? No phones. No Internet. No shops. Not even a place to buy new clothes or shoes. This is child cruelty. Get us back home or you'll be charged with child abuse when they find us."

Raven watched the mood drop again. Hanna's outburst spoke volumes. Then she received critical support.

Zigor said, "Aye, but first we need to find local food. I've eaten emergency space rations. It's like eating shoe leather, only less tasty. I say we scour this place. There must be stuff we can eat. If nothing else, perhaps those caribou are tasty."

"Except we don't have big butchering knives," a Spaniard said.

"We have nothing!" a Scotsman said, stomping on the grass.

Many grumbles arose from all quarters.

"Look, people. We must do something," Koralsky said. "Or we'll all starve. If you don't want to use the shuttles to search for food, then me and my crew will take them."

"Good point," Bain Macnab, the Scottish liaison, said. "We'll all feel better with full stomachs. I say let's go hunting. Who's with me?"

Spurred into action, five groups took off in shuttles. Their departure calmed those remaining behind.

Raven said, "Okay. Why don't we go through all our belongings other than clothing and hygiene items and make a list of what equipment we have with us? Their engineers might recognize something as useful that the rest of us wouldn't. Maybe between us, we'll have enough to make it."

More grumbling followed, but hundreds wandered off to make their lists. Some volunteered to compile the individual lists within each group.

Faith Koralsky pulled Raven Cooper aside. "We ran a skeleton crew this trip. Twenty-four of us. We don't have a group and we're too small. Any chance we can join your group? We'd fit in better with yours."

"Yes, love to have you guys. The more, the better our chances for survival. When I saw the damage, I figured we'd be stranded here. They elected me the group leader or liaison person, but you'll remain in charge of the ship. Er, what about Commander Bloom?"

"Thank you. I don't think he'll—"

The sound of a muffled blaster fire interrupted Faith.

"It came from inside! Come on."

The two raced through the cargo hold into the halls of the ship. Hans caught up with them as he dashed from engineering.

"Someone fired a blaster," he said. "That way."

As they jogged along, others from the bridge joined them.

Julie said, "Sounded like it came from near the commander's quarters."

By the time the XO reached Commander Bloom's cabin, the entire crew had joined them. The Chief of Security reached them last.

He said, "Armory is still secure. Just checked. What's going on? Who fired the blaster?"

Koralsky knocked. "Commander? Are you okay? Open up."

Receiving no reply, she used her pass code.

"Shit! You guys, stay out. Doc, you can check, but I think he's dead."

Doctor Marshall Wu moved past the others and into the cabin, while Raven picked up the blaster from the floor. She handed it to Sam.

"Lock it up in the armory," Koralsky said.

"Aye, sir."

"And get me a complete inventory of all weapons on the ship. The rest of you, we're now part of Raven's group. So fan out. Make a list of every item on the ship that might aid our survival."

Dr. Wu said, "Commander Bloom is dead. Took half his head off."

"I'll see he's taken outside and buried," the Chief of Security said.

"Thanks. Weapons are going to be problematical,"

Koralsky said. “A blaster makes anyone powerful. Take what they want from whomever. Crew, we will follow Raven’s orders when we’re outside the ship, and everyone will follow ours when inside the ship. At least for now.”

Hans said, “XO—”

“Just Faith or Koralsky please.”

He grinned. “Okay, boss.”

The others chuckled or smiled. “Can I enlist the help of some of the security folks? There are a lot of places equipment is stored in this ship. Besides listing it, I’d like to bring the more useful or valuable items to engineering where we can keep them secured. I don’t trust all the group’s people. Some might take to stealing to survive.”

“Excellent. Keep the door secured with the pass code known to you and me only. Things could get desperate. I’ll talk to Raven.”

“I’ll miss the old coot,” Hans said. “He ran the Hawker well for over a decade.”

“Aye,” Julie said, “he had faith in me, giving me this astronomer position when he didn’t have to. He had so much experience to share with us. We need that now more than ever. Why did he have to do that?”

Dr. Wu said, “His health had been declining. He didn’t want it known, but he had a complete physical scheduled when we got back. Heart issues, I suspected. I’ll miss his guidance.”

Another loud noise echoed down the halls.

“Came from the below cabins,” Hans said.

“Sounded like one of those antique guns,” Faith said. “Come on. Just what we need. People going around shooting people. God, this is getting messy fast.”

Raven joined them as they headed down one hallway. “Was that a gunshot?” she asked.

“Think so. Came from a cabin holding some of your group members,” Hans said.

A high-pitched shriek demanded their attention.

“That way,” Faith said.

Upon entering a connecting hallway with cabins lining both sides, one door opened, and Hanna rushed out, screaming. Her brother, Dave, stumbled out after her, dazed. Raven grabbed Hanna and pulled the shrieking teen up to her body, holding her tightly until she quieted.

Faith and the others rushed inside. She stuck her head out.

"Shot himself."

She headed back inside as Raven calmed Hanna down.

"What happened?" she asked.

Hanna broke into a sobbing fit, but Dave spoke up.

"He said we had two choices. Do nothing and die slowly of starvation or let him shoot us. I said we might still get rescued one day, so he shrugged, put his ancient gun to his head, and fired. Blood flew everywhere. Hanna freaked. Pretty disgusting. Some father. Bastard. Loved money. Not us."

A woman from the next cabin came out and overheard what happened.

"Oh, you poor, poor things. Come. I've just made some apple strudels. You kids can stay with us," she said, pulling Hanna from Raven, who hadn't given Hanna or Dave a flood of sympathy.

Turning, Dave said, "When Mom died, we wanted to live with our aunt, but Dad wouldn't let us, and he had all the money. Look where that got him and us. Maybe we should have let him shoot us."

"No, you chose wisely," Raven said. "Life is still within you."

Koralsky said, "I don't regret his absence, but we'll all miss the commander. He is or was like a father to many of us. How could Stroebel do that in front of his own kids?"

As they watched several men carry Stroebel's body outside, she said, "Mark my words, we're likely to see an epidemic of suicides."

Raven sighed. "We must nip this in the bud. We'll hold a burial this evening when everyone's back. I've an idea."

"Glad you do. All I can do is keep the guns locked

up."

As the red orb headed for the western horizon, everyone assembled outside the ship, some distance away from where Hans and several men had dug a large grave. Everyone had heard about the two deaths. Raven found a pastor among the parties and had him say the departing words. She noticed most of the crew had watering eyes, but no one shed a tear over Stroebel's passing. When the pastor finished, Raven got their attention.

"One moment, everyone. In case you don't know me, I'm Raven Cooper, the liaison for the English group. The Hawker's crew have joined us. I want to discuss something with everyone. We need an overall leader to coordinate our actions. I have stepped up to do that for now.

"There is no doubt that our survival is a monumental challenge, but one I'm sure we can achieve. However, as you've just seen, some of us have chosen to not make any effort to survive. These two men gave up. They also gave up on the rest of us, who are doing everything we can to survive and make a new home here on Landfall.

"In killing themselves, both men made life more difficult for the rest of us. I helped Faith clean up the commander's cabin and then Stroebel's cabin. What an awful mess. And even worse, Stroebel's kids watched him blow his brains all over their cabin.

"I suspect many more of you are ready to give up, finding death more appealing than life. And I agree with many of you that to live or die is a personal choice. What I would ask of those who choose to die, please, don't make it harder on the rest of us to clean up after you. Hans and the fellows spent hours digging that grave. Time which could have been better spent on improving our chances of survival.

"During the next three days, those of you wishing to end your life, come see me. I'll put you on a list. Then, in three days, those who've chosen death can do so. We'll do it for you and in a humane and probably painless way—one that does not create a horrid mess for others to clean up afterwards. I hope those of you who are considering this option will change your mind, but I won't override your decision."

While others nodded, a German man spoke up. "My thanks to Miss Cooper for taking on such an enormous responsibility. Gerde and I have adopted Stroebel's kids for now. We must have one person to go to for many things. Someone who's smart, which Miss Cooper is. But I'd like to ask her one question. Are we just deluding ourselves? That we can somehow survive this? Make a good life here out of absolutely nothing?"

Raven felt thousands of eyes drilling her. Utter silence. She sighed.

"God, people! Trying to make a livable world out of nothing is the *greatest* challenge we'll ever face. I'm alive. I want to live. We have seeds and animals and people. We still have the ship for now. But it *us* who'll determine our success or failure. I'm a physicist and was about to teach high school physics to many young minds. I still want to teach. We all have skills vital to our survival. Farmers know how to farm. I know nothing about horses, cows, and chickens. You do. Between us, we have the knowledge. Whether we have the drive to succeed is yet to be seen.

"Didn't we all embark on this journey in hopes of making a better world and life for ourselves and our families? It's not New Terra. It's Landfall. Yes, it's going to take all of us to turn this vast nothingness into a vibrant world. The future is ours to make. I will die trying to make it into a world I'm proud to live on. We can do this if we all work together. Thank you."

Quite unexpectedly, Koralsky began slow-clapping. Soon, other hands joined her, causing Raven to blush.

When the crowd dispersed, Faith said, "Terrific speech. Thanks. You said what needed to be said."

When the three days ended, twelve men and women chose death. At least they helped dig their own graves. One by one, Koralsky fired a blaster shot into their heads and pushed their bodies into the large hole.

"Now I truly am a murderer," she whispered to Raven, who stood by her side.

"No, you're not. You allowed them their way out in such a way as to not burden the rest of us. And Doctor Wu confiscated valuable pills from some of them."

Chapter 7 Getting Organized

"Look what we found," Ingel Stroebel said. "Gold nuggets and silver, too! Those mountains to the east are loaded with them. We picked up these along some streams that feed into that river we're calling Middle Fork. We can't eat them, but we can use them as a means of exchange."

Raven said, "The German group didn't bring any livestock or fowl onboard. This gives them something to exchange with those who did. 'I'll take a skein of wool for six eggs' won't work."

Rafael roared. "Good point. We can't go around trading a horse for a cow. Stuff like that. We need an acceptable means of exchange. You are good, Raven."

"More than that," Ingel said, "we caught these." His partner held up a string of fish. "The Middle Fork River is loaded with these. Could have filled the shuttle if we'd had proper fishing gear with us. Tomorrow, we'll catch enough for everyone."

Poppy Norton said, "We visited that small group of mountains where the two rivers join. We found flocks of these furry animals that look sort of like rabbits. We're going to see if they are edible and if they taste good tonight. But we also found tuber plants. Sort of like carrots or maybe turnips. The scanner device says they are edible, so we'll try them with the rabbit-things."

Finlay Macintosh said, "We found nut trees. Thousands of them. We tested some on the ground. Likely last season's. And they're edible. Rather akin to pecans and walnuts. Couple different types."

"How'd you get all those red welts on your face?" Poppy asked.

He flushed. "Our second find. Honey. Lots of it. Brought back a cup to sample. Bees didn't like it, though. If we could build hives, I think we'd be swimming in honey. Spotted a zillion bees around the many nut trees just beginning to flower. Must be spring here."

Several cheered.

"In the southern grasslands," said Miguel Garcia, "we found three different species of berry vines. Just as prickly as Earths. Some will be reddish, some bluish, and some pretty dark. Device says all are edible once they ripen. More of those rabbit-like creatures are there and going after the berries."

Benat Ugarte said, "We went way west into the rolling hills and found hawk-like birds of prey. And many of these." His buddies carried out a new animal. "It's like a goat, we think. Something like that. Eats the grasses. We'll see if it roasts up tonight. If so, there's a lot of them in those rolling hills."

Raven said, "A very well done to all of you. Looks like there is plenty of food out there, if we can catch or pick it. Let's get together tonight and plan out food sorties. At last, we have good news. No one is going to starve to death. Fill me in on how these things taste. I'll keep a record for everyone. And map where we find them."

"Hey, that'll help. Then we'll all know what food possibilities are where. Now if we only had fishing tackle," Ingel said.

"Hey, this is sure weird. Red sun is up, but it's nighttime," Raven said.

Julie and Adrian both began to answer at the same time. He backed off and let her explain.

"Landfall—that's what we are calling this world—our world. It takes twenty days to go around that red sun, so ten of those days, the red sun will shine in the daytime with the yellow sun, but like now, the other ten days, the red sun will shine during the nighttime from the yellow sun. Strange, isn't it? Going to take some getting used to. What worries me is what is winter going to be like when we're much farther away from the hotter yellow sun? Adrian and I think Landfall will have brutal winters. Guess we'll see."

Raven said, "We should make a map of our continent and give these places names. My name for the planet has stuck. Landfall. What should we call those giant mountains of the far north?"

"Helades," someone yelled. Another named the thick forest abutting it to the south of the Dark Forest, because the trees there were dense and dark, a kind of evergreen they guessed. The mountains at the western edge of the continent became known as the Lower Helades, because they appeared to be an extension of the northern range. That patch of forest nestled between the two ranges there at the northeast corner became the Black Forest. Between these two dense woods lay the land of many lakes, which Dusty named the Lake District, a reminder of home. The long river that ran down the middle of the continent from the Helades to the swamp and delta at the southern edges became the Land River.

The long east-west river to the north became the North Fork River, while the similar river further south became the Middle Fork, and the southern one became the South Fork. All three joined the Land River. The picturesque smaller mountains in the middle where the Land and North Fork met became the Lesser Helades. Three Peaks became the name of the smaller mountains between the Middle Fork and the Southern Fork. These lay close to where the Hawker had landed.

The vivid red sands of the desert at the extreme southeastern section of the continent became the Red Desert. Rolando Hills became the name of the vast hills of the western section. The Southern Grasslands became the name of the land north of the South Fork, while Northern Grasslands became the name of the land above the Middle Fork. They called the swampy delta Verde Swamp.

The next day, Raven used a computer to create a map, adding rough distance measurements. She guessed square-shaped Landfall was about three thousand miles a side, perhaps more. She printed off copies for every family, hundreds of copies. *I've made communications about destinations easier to handle. But the only way to get to most of these places is via one of the five shuttles. Gonna need to solve this one soon.*

As she handed out the maps, she said, “We need some kind of transportation vehicles to make use of what’s out there. Think of ideas.”

Over breakfast, the five leaders met, insisting Koralsky join them.

Raven said, “We all agree that laying in food supplies is our first objective. We can quarter in the Hawker over the coming year, which requires a water supply. Faith has said we’ve about drained the ship’s water supply. If we are going to have any crops this year, we best get the seeds planted. That means plowing some of the grassland here. But we have no farming equipment.”

Rafael said, “We didn’t bring along any work horses, but perhaps we could rig up some ways for horses to pull a plow, if we had a plow.”

“I can have Hans fabricate a plow-like tool by cannibalizing part of the ship,” Koralsky said. “Unfortunately, most of the ship is aluminum alloy, not steel.

Ingel Stroebel, the new leader of the German group, said, “We’re going to need steel for many things. Axes, saws, plows, hammer, horseshoes. The list is endless. I can have my people look for iron deposits. If we can find some, perhaps we can set up a foundry to make steel. Does anyone know how steel is made?”

No one responded.

“Normally, the geologist on a deep space exploration ship would do a thorough mineralogy survey of a new world,” Koralsky said. “I think I can outfit a shuttle with the equipment to do that. Then, we’d know better where we stand. Do we have coal or oil deposits? That would be useful to know. Can we make use of geothermal electricity generation? Eventually, the small nuclear reactor that runs life support will run out of fuel. After that, no electricity, but I think that won’t happen for at least a year or more. We have time.”

Raven said, “From what I’ve seen of the rivers on Landfall, hydroelectric power generation is a no-go.”

“Lazy rivers,” Rafael said, and everyone chuckled.

"We should build better shelters for the animals before winter comes," Zigor said. "Don't think we want to share the Hawker with them all winter long."

"No way," Bain Macnab said, "but we'll need to harvest our sheep's wool by next spring. That will yield volumes of wool from which we can make clothes."

"That's the one thing our computer is good at," Koralsky said. "We have an extensive database. We should research how that's done. Get some women who are good with material looking into ways and means. I've seen weavers using a loom once. It can be done."

"Methods of building shelters and water wells should be our next priority, once we get the crops planted and regular food deliveries going," Raven said. "What about making ropes? We'll need rope along with ways to make these shelters."

"I saw a log cabin once," Bain said. "No idea how they built it without nails. If we had lots of rocks, we could make stone buildings. I can't believe we don't even have tools to quarry stone. This is the pits! How can we possibly survive?"

Many grumbles echoed his question. Raven changed tone.

"Guys, the ancient Egyptians built the pyramids, and they didn't have steel, either. We just need to be more inventive. Let's get the mineralogy survey done. Then, we can tell better what resources we have. Meantime, let's lay out planting fields, get a better water supply, and build up our food supplies before we must eat that blue goo stuff."

They divided up to get their people to work on the current projects. Sabrina Norton took charge of laying out the farming plots, ten in number. She and her crew experimented on ways to clear the grass and plow, which yield little other than extensive effort. However, Lyn Riggs had a bright idea. Using a butcher knife borrowed from the galley, she cut a rectangular block and pulled the sod up.

"Hey, here's a sod brick. Soil is much easier to work underneath. Come on. Let's cut sod bricks."

As they stacked the bricks up, Dusty suggested they

could build a sort of shelter from them. Thus began the first sod barn shelter.

When asked to help with the ground preparation work for the farms, Hanna Stroebel said, "But that's for the others to do. I won't damage my nails cause there's no nail salon around here. Unless you know of one. You can't make us."

"Isn't that what workers are for?" Dave asked. "We're Stroebels."

Dusty didn't know what to say to the kids and turned to Raven. "Frankly, if they were my kids, I'd paddle their rears, but that's gone so out of fashion."

Raven sighed and looked at the two kids whose father had committed suicide not ten days ago. Spoiled brats. "Okay, Hanna, Dave. Here's the situation. We're stranded on an uncivilized planet without basic survival tools. You have two choices. One, shut the fuck up and help with the garden plots, or two, don't help us and get by on your own."

"I'll take two," Hanna said, glaring at her.

"Excellent choice. I'll spread the word. No one will provide you with food or water. Those will be yours to get. Mind you, if you steal them, Koralsky won't hesitate to throw you in the brig. There's fish in the rivers and berries down south and rabbit-things are everywhere. Go to it. Make sure you thoroughly cook them. You don't want to get worms, since we don't have any de-worming medicines. Bye."

"Wait. You can't do that. We have to eat," Dave said.

"Everyone is doing their part to help us survive. You two want no part of it, so you aren't allowed to eat what we contribute each day. The South Fork is the closest river. Maybe fifty miles south. Best be on your way if you want to eat."

Hanna said, "But this is hopeless work. Nothing's going to grow here. Too damned cold. We inherited Dad's fortune, so we'll pay for our food."

"That would work perfectly if we were on Earth. But I don't see any banks around here," Raven said, waving her arms across the expanse of grasslands. "So be my guest and make your cash withdrawals. When you hand me the credits, you'll get supper."

"You can't do this to us!" Hanna insisted.

"Everyone else knows they must contribute. Unless you can find some way off this world and back to Earth, you must contribute to the survival of everyone to receive our help. Don't expect anyone to help you if you are unwilling to help others. I'm sorry you've led such a spoiled life, but that's over now."

The two stormed over to Jurgen Kaiser, who'd begun laying the foundation of the first barn-like shelter. They handed him the sod bricks he needed.

Raven then focused her attention on how to get a water supply to the ship. The only reasonable way had to be a well, since she expected the winters would be frigid. She headed off to find the XO.

"Hi. I've got more problems than I can solve, but no one else is doing it. What are we going to do about water supply? We need a nearby well, but we've no well digging machines."

"You're doing an outstanding job with keeping us all organized and focused on the tasks at hand," the XO said. "Know what you mean, though. I'm so glad I could give up being the ship's leader. Any alternative ideas how to drill a well? It's a deep hole, isn't it?"

Raven bit her lip. "Hum, do you have any disintegrators in your armory?"

Koralsky's eyes widened. "What do you want them for? Have we got more troubles?"

"No, I want to use them to dig a well. I studied their power output and ranges in college. I'm thinking they might vaporize the ground. I know that's not their intended targets, but..."

"Now that's the wildest idea I've ever heard. Come on. I'll unlock them for you. We carry only a dozen. We've mostly blasters. Say, we've got a 50mm disintegrator cannon topside. It's for drilling holes in enemy ships."

Unfortunately, it's position on the top of the ship

prevented aiming directly at the ground. Hence, Koralsky and Raven spent several days dismantling it and making a portable tripod for it. They picked an ideal spot from where piping into the ship could be done. She let Faith fire the weapon. Wearing goggles, she pulled the trigger. Giant plumes of dust and vaporized debris rose, obscuring vision. She kept the continuous firing going until the gun needed recharging.

When the air cleared, the two saw a perfectly formed hole. They measured its depth at about one hundred feet, but water filled the last twenty feet. It fell to Hans to rig up an electric pump that filled up the internal water tanks. Soon, they discovered they only needed to run the pump once a week to replenish the ship's onboard water supply. Raven felt confident water wouldn't be a problem going forward.

Hans said, "Raven, you're an absolute genius!"

Chapter 8 Survey Says...

"Freezing rain and snow," Dusty complained the day after the two suns rose above Landfall. "I thought this spring."

"I think it has something to do with both suns not up concurrently," Julie said. "Makes the nighttime actually dark, unlike what it was a couple of days ago. I think we'll just have to get used to the crazy weather. Wonder what winters will be like."

"Oh, don't even mention winters! My poor chickens aren't liking this weather."

Despite the weather, the five shuttles returned.

Ingel Stroebel's huge smile suggested he'd found what he wanted.

"We found a large deposit of iron cradled up against the Lower Helades at the far eastern edge of the Northern Grasslands. There's also veins of almost pure copper. Lead and zinc are mixed with silver ores. It's a miner's paradise."

Rafael explained his findings. "There are large coal deposits in southern Rolando Hills and a peat bog near the Verde Swamp. The hill country is ideal horse land."

"We found an exposed granite deposit, ready-made for mining slabs. If only we had a way to carve out blocks. Also, came across a large section of mica sheets that could be used for windows. Sheep would do well up there, too," Bain said.

Poppy said, "And we ventured closer to the Red Desert. We found clay suitable for making ceramic pots. We're going to need lots of pots to store things. Of course, there's a lot of sand, if and when we get into glass making. Now if we only had wagons to bring stuff back."

Hans said, "I've gone over the ship and worked out what we forge tools from or create tools from or mold into tools. I'm assuming we're all staying onboard this winter. I can supply aluminum alloy tools soon. Axes, shovels, knives, along with buckets will come first. Oh, and we've got the new well going, thanks to Raven's bright idea. All restrictions on shower lengths are lifted. Just don't use all the hot water."

"Working together is proving successful," Raven said, thanking them.

"But I want to take our people up to the mining area," Ingel said. "The sooner we get to mining and smelting, the sooner we can produce proper tools. Trouble is, there's no way to transport five hundred of us and our things up there."

"And no place to stay when you get there," Raven said.

"True. So I was thinking maybe we could ferry a couple dozen of us up there. They could construct crude shelters and get a start on mining. The sooner we can get a forge roaring, the sooner we can make anvils and then proper tools," Ingel said.

Poppy said, "Hey, drop some of us off down south at the clay deposits. We can spend several days ferrying back a lot of it and then make the pots we'll need."

"My people are eager to make bee hives. We could have a large supply of honey by winter if someone can fell a few trees," Zigor said.

"Hey," Bain said, "We also found a huge salt flat. We're a need'n that, lassies."

"And the caribou are providing us with hides and bone tools," Vera Basarte said. "We want to borrow a blaster or two to bring several down. The one we did yesterday cooked up well, much like venison. We can make warm clothing from their hides, and Zigor thinks we might tame and ride them. They certainly aren't afraid of us."

"And Julie and I've gotten a handle on the weather patterns," Adrian said. "It is a temperature differential driving the wild weather. When the red sun sets as the yellow sun rises, it creates a swing in temperatures. That happens twice during the 20-day red sun year. It also happens when the red sun just begins to rise as the yellow sun rises. These create the heat differential, which causes these wild swings in the weather. Expect wild weather occurring three days out of the twenty days of the red sun year. Strong winds, heavy rains, and probably heavy snows in the winters, based on the freezing rains we've experienced. The effect only lasts about two days. So six days out of the twenty days in the month we can expect bad weather."

Doctor Kelly Johnson grumbled. "That's fine, but we're missing vital points. You've six doctors among us. We have only the surgery bay in the ship to treat the seriously injured. Once the ship's medical supplies are used up, we've no more of anything. Bandages, medications, antibiotics, surgical tools. Nothing. How are we doctors to treat you when you get injured or sick? And it's worse. What about dentists? There are none. So what do you do about cavities? Root canals? Broken teeth? How are we supposed to care for your dental needs? This whole 'let's survive this' is going nowhere."

Jen Klein, the German vet, said, "And what about us vets? How do you expect us to service your animals without equipment, facilities, or medicines? Worse, there are only four of us vets. So what happens when one of our doctors or vets dies? Who will replace them? Twenty years from now, it's likely you will have zero medical people left. Survey says this whole thing is becoming an utterly pointless exercise in futility. We're doomed. Might not die next week or next month. But I wouldn't give a rat's ass for anyone being alive in fifty years, unless they are living like cave men."

Bill Warden spoke up. "Survey says we found cave systems. Sabrina Norton and I took one shuttle up to the Dark Forest, looking for the source of the Land River. We found an extensive cave systems good for wintering shelter, but the distance from the ship is a problem. Didn't find the river's source, though. Not yet."

Zigor said, "Hey, we should mark these new finds on our maps. We really like the cave discovery."

Lyn Shepherd volunteered her findings. "Some of us came across deceased birds. After boiling the flesh off, their tiny bones will make excellent needles, if we can find a way to drill eye holes in them. Maybe the doctors could use them to sew up wounds. It's a start, anyway."

Raven countered the depressive spell the doctor had cast over the group. She said, "Survey says we won't be dying anytime soon. When we first landed here, many figured we would be dead in days. Now, we've pushed our demise off by at least twenty years. Don't quit on us yet. A year from now, we might have altered that doom prediction to a hundred years."

"Don't count on it," Doctor Wu said. "Gerde Howe is a diabetic. She has about fifty days before our insulin supply is exhausted. After that, she'll be dead in short order. If anyone comes down with a serious illness, you're doomed as well."

Raven grimaced, but had to change the mood somehow. "You heard him. So you guys, don't go getting sick."

That produced a mixture of chuckles and snickers. But the mood lightened a little.

Then, Zigor broached a subject Raven dreaded. "Since XO Koralsky is here, I've a question. Each group wants to settle in a different area. The Germans, up in the mining country, for example. When we do split off, will we divide everything into five equal parts? Specifically, the ship's valuable supplies, like weapons and shuttles."

"Would that mean we'd get some horses and sheep?" Ingel asked.

"And chickens?" Rafael asked. "Do we divide up everything into equal parts? Even the things each of our groups brought along for New Terra? I'm not inclined to give up the horses we brought. I don't think Zigor wants to part with his cattle or Bain, his sheep. But the ship—now that's a whole different story. It seems to me they owe each group an equal share, seeing how we're stranded here because of the ship. No offense, XO Koralsky."

Faith ran her hands over her face before replying. "Yes, that would be the honorable approach. But keep in mind shuttles need fuel, which we've been taking from the ion engines supplies, and blasters need recharging. Hans is cutting up the metal framework for tools. He'll see each group gets an equal share. Honestly, a year from now, there likely won't be anything left of use to us, and the metal will be more valuable than the blasters or shuttles, especially when the fuel supply is exhausted."

Ingel said, "Rafael, for us to move everything, we'll need horses. Surely we can devise some equitable trade."

Horse trading began, though no one intended to move just yet.

Then Bain said, "By my calculations, a yellow sun year is twenty of the red sun months. Astronomers, don't we have like another fifteen months until fall and winter come? Plenty of time to handle moving and building homes, perhaps. Something to ponder, anyway."

When the group dispersed, chatting among themselves, Faith pulled Raven aside.

"You know, there's another aspect no one's mentioned. Babies."

Raven said, "Yeah, I know. I've been doing population calculations. Any way that you look at it, we'll need a lot of children going forward."

"Ah, you've thought of that. Ace and I have had a bit of a fling, but I don't want to be tied down in a marriage. Like you, I like my freedom of action. But I suppose I could have a baby or so, as long as I wouldn't be tied down with it for years. How about you?"

Raven smiled. "Sex isn't as wonderful as people claim. When I was eighteen, I did it once with a guy I rather liked. Messy, disgusting, and certainly not enjoyable. Was for him, though. At least he said so. But you're right. The long-term survival of this group depends on having an abundance of children. Without proper medical care, it could well be parallel to the Dark Ages, where half the children born never survive into adulthood." She sighed. "I'm resigned to having them. Don't mind teaching them. In fact, I look forward to being a teacher. So I'll just have to endure a man doing his thing once in a while. Just enough to get me pregnant."

"You and I are alike in many ways. When folks decide to break up into households, how about you and I teaming up? I think I can talk Ace into being our stud when needed and maybe looking after us some. I mean, when we are bloated blimps for a time."

"You got a deal!"

"I wonder what skills I can bring to the English group?" Faith asked. "I'm a commanding officer in the Space Force. That's all I know, that and piloting ships and navigation. I'm not cut out to be a farmer."

"No, you're a leader. A take-charge person. We'll need you to help manage the workers when the time comes. You'll fit right in, Faith. Besides, I'm sure our group is staying here. With the ship. Even after the other groups split for their ideal locations, someone needs to stay close to the ship. Medical facilities and other things will still need to be available when needed. I'm thinking we might convert part of the ship into a school for everyone. Besides, it is pretty here being so close to those Three Peaks. Picturesque."

"I'm going to allow cannibalization of the ship's bedding when they leave. That's one thing we have in abundance. Sheets and blankets and single person beds. Some could be made into clothing? I'm going to see what else we have stashed away in cubbyholes."

Chapter 9 Moving Forward

The five group heads met one after the two suns graced the daytime skies and the stormy weather abated.

Ingel Stroebel said, "We make our move now and claim the region up north and stop the Basques form getting there first. If we wait a year, what's stopping you Basques from getting there first? Landfall has a bountiful food supply."

"Aye, that looks like a very profitable location," Zigor said. "And our cattle could do just as well up there. But shouldn't we wait a year, staying here as Raven suggests?"

"I like the idea of nearly unlimited wealth," Rafael said. "And we have the horses to get us to the mining country in force. But it is farther north, and we don't know the severity of Landfall's winters yet. Raven has a point. Shouldn't we establish basic industries first?"

"Homes, barns, and water wells," Bain Macnab said. "Do we really want to isolate ourselves from the others by a thousand miles? On Earth, our peoples had little interaction, except Zigor and Rafael's groups lived near each other. We planned to go our own ways once we landed on New Terra. But here, we have nothing. We're on our own."

"That's my point, fellows," Raven said, after listening to them and feeling out the groups views. "We could build a small town right here, enough for twenty-five hundred of us. Get our industries established. And learn what curve balls this world has in store. Strength in numbers. I know Stroebel's people want to claim the mining lands up north. But think about the situation, Ingel. You have maybe five hundred men, women, and children in your group. That's your worker pool for home building, food production and mining operations. Tall order for so few people.

"Here, we've only completed one sod barn structure, but need hundreds of homes. I think the wisest move we could make is to agree on which group lays claim to what part of Land, but let's all work together here at Three Peaks and build a town, which we can use as a base of future operations."

"She has a point," Rafael said. "My people are tired of cramped crew cabins. What we'd give for a proper bed. Besides, what if the winters are harsh? Deep snow. We need to have laid in a goodly supply of food beforehand. Northern Spanish winters limit foraging. The Pyrenees can be unforgiving in winters."

Raven said, "Hans has been cutting up the ship and making axes and hammers. Maybe we can focus on logging trees for houses. That alone would raise morale. Plus, how will we feed all the animals come winter?"

Several men flushed, and she knew she'd scored.

"She has a point," Rafael said. "The horses and cows need shelter and winter hay. As you've seen, in days, they turn fenced areas into mud lots. And we don't know the length of Landfall winters."

Shrugs answered him.

Rafael said, "Any ideas how we can and make hay for the winter without a tractor, cutter, raker, and bailer?"

Raven pulled up the ship's computer database and searched for ideas for Rafael and Zigor on how to make hay.

She said, "Without a bailer, haystacks are our only option."

As a result of this, Hans fashioned scythe blades, which some of Zigor's men attached to wooden shafts. Others crafted wooden pitchforks. And slow but steady harvesting of taller grasses began.

Men felled trees using aluminum axes Hans made from the ship's thick angle beams. Others stripped branches from tree trunks and chopped them into firewood for winter, the younger folk stacking them into piles.

A woman worked out a way to make crude ropes,

allowing horse power to be used for hauling the logs to construction sites. Soon, the men standardized cabins twenty-foot square. Bain's people gathered large rocks and worked out a mortar mix using clay brought up from the south intended for pottery. Before long, the frame of the first house with an internal fireplace rose above the grasslands. Plexiglass salvaged from the ship worked as windows. Hinges for the door came from the ship as well.

Children filled cracks in the logs with mud, thinking it great fun. Men worked building the roof while women stomped-down grass inside for flooring until one had the idea to use mud bricks instead. Soon the women worked at making mud bricks and setting them out to dry.

Two weeks later, after another bout of stormy weather, they finished the first house. Koralsky and Raven drilled a new water well for the house using the 50mm disintegrator cannon. The men built stone walls around the well to prevent accidental fall-ins. Raven noted how much this project raised morale. And with eagerness, they began work on another house and winter shelter.

Bella Vega dropped by to talk with Raven.

"Thanks for seeing me. I'm something of a mathematician. Has anyone brought up the fact that long-term survival here requires many more children? And with as many fathers as possible to spread the gene pool around? Not all women with us can bear more children. If each who still can has four children with four fathers, then the next generation can get by with three children each, barring any unforeseen catastrophe. After that, the numbers can vary. If we don't have four in this generation, the odds of anyone left alive in a hundred years is not even fifty-fifty. And if we don't broaden the gene pool, those who are born that far down the line will suffer genetic complications in later generations due to inbreeding like it did with the Hapsburgs of history or the ancient Egyptians."

"I knew we'd need a solution but had no idea of accurate figures. I don't know the actual breeding facts."

"Well, I do. I've not mentioned it before because

some of us are happily married and would frown on extra-marital affairs. Before we got stranded here, I would have divorced him if he'd played around. But now, there's a need to re-examine our feelings and positions."

"Makes sense. Plus, some of us women would prefer not to be married. But I also realize survival depends on having more children. So I'm not opposed to bearing them via various fathers, but I prefer not to be tied down by marriage."

"That would work perfectly, Raven. It's simply a matter of the number of children with a wide variety of genes."

"But I think before we encourage pregnancy, we should have homes built and a steady supply of food."

She sighed. "Yes, you're right, as usual. Some are calling you the Goddess of Landfall. You always know the right thing to say and do."

"Thanks for your vote of confidence."

Sounds of fighting drew Raven and Koralsky outside from their town planning desk. Dozens of men brawled, fists bashing bodies all around the outside of the ship. Using her wrist comm set, Koralsky called for Captain Smeltzer to bring out the stun guns and a blaster.

"Oh, shit!" he said, handing the blaster to her while priming the stun gun.

Blam. She fired a charge into the air, and the blast got everyone's attention.

"Stop fighting right now or be stunned," she yelled into the sudden silence, which was only momentary, as several men threw one last punch. Of course, those hit had to retaliate. The brawl continued, as Sam handed out stun guns to the rest of his security forces as they arrived on the scene.

Standing side by side, they moved forward, firing at any fighters in front of them. The shock forced each man to collapse, momentarily paralyzed. With calm restored, the XO discovered they had raided the alcoholic beverages and consumed all the ship's stores of beer and hard spirits, which she guessed triggered the fight among over a hundred men.

"Way to go, guys. You've used up all our beer and liquor," she said at the top of her voice. "No more beer until the supply ships come."

"Eh, when is that?" one drunk man lying on the ground blurted out.

"I'd throw you all in the brig, but it only holds two people. Clean up the mess. And carry those empty beer kegs back into the ship."

Raven watched the drunkards staggering about, trying to move the empty kegs, while she stifled laughter. She looked at Koralsky. And the two burst out laughing.

"Well, that'll never happen again. Good riddance," the XO said.

Bella Vega asked, "Don't you want to know who started it?"

"Nope. Now we have no beer or hard liquor to worry about."

Bella tried to offer a 'but,' as Koralsky and Cooper walked off.

"The real question," Koralsky said, "is how long this many men stay civil while cooped up for months during the winter? Ah, storms coming. The red sun has set, and it's barely morning. We should make our plans around half the time being stormy."

"I'll miss not having milk and eggs for breakfast once they go their separate ways," Raven said.

Late that afternoon, Benat Ugarte dropped off five new bee hives he'd crafted.

"I've made five for each group. This way, everyone can benefit from honey. I love bees. People, not so much."

She thanked him.

"I don't think everyone will stay through the year. Heard lots of talk. The fight today—many can't stand the Germans and their aloofness."

Things did not improve after the drunken brawl. The Basques, Spaniards, and Scotts often made snide remarks at the Germans who belittled them. Only Raven's English group seemed immune to the bickering.

As the daytime temperatures rose, so did the arguments.

Chapter 10 Two Discoveries

As the climate moved into the summer months, outlooks changed. Not a people-person, Benat Ugarte took pleasure in long walks away from the ship. On one of his journeys to the Three Peaks, he discovered something that sent him jogging back to the ship to tell others, finding Zigor, first, who took him to see Raven Cooper right away.

"Benat here discovered something at Three Peaks you ought to come see. Pure copper. Yeah, a vein of pure copper."

Within minutes, Koralsky fired up a shuttle. She flew Raven and the two men over to the Three Peaks to check this out. As she approached the location that Benet pointed out, all the instruments on her control panel danced about like drunken men on a random walk.

"Is the altitude thing broken?" Raven asked, frowning. "They're all going crazy."

"I'm flying by the sight, not the instruments. They've gone bonkers. Never seen anything like this before. No, now they're acting normal again. How weird is that?"

"Benat says down there," Zigor said from the rear seat.

Faith landed the shuttle on the grasslands leading up to the up-thrusting peaks, which looked as though some god had pushed three identical mountains up from deep underground.

"Over here," Benat said, leading them to his discovery.

The four stared at the vein of shining copper streaking across the rocky ground up to the peaks. The vein measured a foot across. The exposed vein ran for several hundred feet before disappearing under the grasslands at one end and underneath the uplifted twisted layers of metamorphic rock that formed the Three Peaks, which displayed sparking mica bits among the multicolored layers, creating a visual wonderland.

Weathering of the surrounding rock allowed them to break off chunks. They pried off several chucks of copper to take back. But the shuttle didn't make more than a hundred feet before the electronic controls acted up again. Curious, Koralsky sat the shuttle down. A close inspection revealed the top of a nearby meteorite made of iron with unusually strong electro-magnetic properties, which had caused the low-flying shuttle's instruments to malfunction.

"That's a source of ready-made iron. I'll send men back to get it," Koralsky said. "Benat, well done on finding that copper!"

Later, the meteorite weighed in at over fifty pounds. Using a thin-beam disintegrator gun, Hans cut it into five equal portions, one for each group. Raven's group made arrow heads and knives for butchering from theirs.

During the next two weeks of good weather, the builders constructed another house identical to the first one, and Ace transported copper from the Three Peaks for others to work. On one of these trips, he discovered a unique rock quarry site. Here, the rock intrusion had formed into rectangular sections. Using a disintegrator gun, he made a cut at the base of one block, freeing a several hundred pound block. Ace thought he could use it in the construction of a stone castle, fortress, or building.

He returned the next day, ferrying the personal lifter machine, which his crew sometimes used to load heavy cargo or shuttles into or out of the ship. With it, he could move the stone with ease. Ace removed another dozen blocks and began building a rock wall. Next day, he brought Koralsky and Raven to see his creation.

"We could easily build a castle or a fortress or a really solid building, one that would last for ages."

"Stone would also act as insulation," Raven said. "I like this idea. There is an ample supply of usable stone here. I wonder how it formed? Wish we had a geologist with us."

"If we build here, there's no need to transport the stone, and the weight of it will stand on solid rock. Built to last, I'd say. We have six personal lifters and several cranes. With rechargeable disintegrators, we could build whatever you wanted here."

Raven gave the okay for Ace and a dozen of his group to clear enough ground to verify the underlying rock base could be used in this way. While they did that, Faith looked for images of stone buildings, while Raven made sketches of some, using the measurements of Ace's original stone blocks.

When the men returned, Ace reported the site as ideal. "Two hundred feet to the south, the intrusion plunged deep underground. It's relatively flat on top. The flat plateau is three hundred feet across, but miles long before it also plunges far underground. If we wanted to build a strong fortress, there's no other better place. It's ideal."

"Okay. Look at some designs we've come up with," Raven said. "I like the idea of retaining the ability to add floors later on, assuming we can make lifting cranes. Faith has found images of what cranes might have looked like back in the Dark Ages."

They discussed which design to use far into the night before reaching a decision. However, that decision altered the next afternoon. When the shuttles returned bringing food and salt supplies, Ingel Stroebel's crew had found a series of caves in Minen Land, ready-made to move in, or so the men said. Likewise, Bain's group brought word of caves in the extreme western edge of the impassible Helades, right next to the Dark Forest. With grasslands to the south, they claimed it would be perfect for sheep and people. And after the brawls, many thought it wise to move.

Amid these ongoing actions, Dr. Marshal Wu paid a visit to Raven.

"No, I'm not here to give you a checkup. Unless you want one. I'm here at the request of the other medical personnel. We might have a health problem on Landfall."

"Please, have a seat. I was just making a cup of tea. Want some?" Over two streaming mugs, she said, "I don't know how long we'll have the luxury of tea. Others are already complaining about the coffee restrictions."

"That's me. Can't survive the mornings without it. I hope someone discovers coffee beans on Landfall somewhere."

"So, what's the problem?"

"It's the makeup of the fine whitish dust that's in the air. It's all over anything left outside overnight."

"I figured it was just dust."

"It's a strange form of organic phosphorous we've never encountered. As a result, we're unsure how it effects humans. Since the stuff is everywhere, it'll be impossible to avoid getting it in our systems."

"So it's not like you want to warn everyone about it?"

"Right. We're watching for unusual symptoms in the population. New world means new threats from bacteria and viruses. We're keeping an eye out for unusual aches, pains, illnesses, that sort of thing. So far, whatever this world has isn't causing our bodies any significant illnesses. Fingers crossed."

"Is there any evidence this phosphorous substance has entered our bodies? Like in our lungs?"

"Astute observation, Miss Cooper. Yes, that's what has raised my concern level. It's shown up in many nasal swabs when we do routine checkups. But it's also present in two blood samples out of the hundred I've taken. Both have concerned me. Absorption within the lungs could explain how it has gotten into blood streams, although not entirely. Further studies are needed, and I felt I needed to keep you abreast of a potential problem."

"Thanks. Excellent work. Damn white stuff seems everywhere. It's been reported everywhere except in the Helades and Lower Helades. Must not come from the mountains. I will see if any plant people can figure where the white organic material originates. If it harms our bodies, we are doomed unless you can find a cure for it."

"That also bothers me. We're not equipped for such studies. No laboratories. If it makes us sick, there's not a lot us doctors can do for victims. Just thought you ought to know."

"Is there any data on this material in your medical field, like from another planet in the Federation? It may not be indigenous to Landfall."

"Not in the ship's database. Unfortunately, we cannot search the Internet."

"Most unfortunate. That. Okay. Keep me posted and I'll try to isolate the source of the material."

Raven checked with Koralsky and Hans about the particles, explaining their doctor had discovered the material in noses and the blood of two people.

Koralsky said, "So it's likely in their lungs, too."

"I assume the ship has some kind of filtration system," Raven said.

Faith shrugged, but Hans said, "Yes. I've not checked the filters since last year's check. Come on. Let's go see."

He led them to the rear section of the cruiser. "Ah, here we are," he said as he removed a panel and pulled out a three-foot square filter. Three sets of eyes stared at the fine white powder-like substance on one side of the filter. "Is this your contaminant?"

"Think so. Let me take some samples," Raven said.

"Do we have replacement filters?" Faith asked.

"Nope. Those were due to be serviced during the retrofit. Best I can to is dust them off and put them back in."

"Do that outside, please," Faith said.

Hans rolled his eyes, grinning.

"So this means we're not immune from this organic compound here inside the ship. That's a lot of accumulation," Raven said, sealing a plastic baggy with a sample.

"As long as this dirt isn't harmful, it's just dirt. We get dirt everywhere except special clean rooms where you wear spacesuits inside," Faith said. "By the way, Ace is excited about building his castle. He's nuts about those ancient structures and once took me to tour one in a small European country. He's become a man with a new purpose, since he's never going to pilot ships again. Not unless we can invent a hyper drive engine."

Hans said, "Yeah, he's had me pull all those personal lifters units out of cold storage. And he's confiscated our three mobile cranes. Good thing they are solar powered. Is he really building a castle?"

"Something like that," Raven said. "He sure seems excited about it."

Faith laughed. "That's all he's been talking about since you okayed his project. Even if it doesn't prove fruitful, you've given him a new purpose for living. Navigator Warden has taken up studying astronomy under Julie and Adrian's tutelage. My crew is adapting to being marooned on this world."

Chapter 11 The Split

Another brawl broke out between the German group and the Basques, but the Scotts joined in on the Basques' side. The English and Spanish groups stayed on the sidelines, though that didn't stop some in Rafael's group from cheering on the Basques. Once again, XO Koralsky broke up the fights by firing a blaster into the air.

"Next person to throw a punch gets shot," she barked.

A German sucker-punched a Basque, who doubled over. Koralsky didn't hesitate, surprising Raven, who came out to see the event. If you blinked, you'd have missed it. One moment, the man had his head, and the next moment, a headless body slumped to the ground.

"Anyone else doubt me? Good. That's enough fighting. Now break it up. Ingel, bury your man," she said, before pivoting and returning to the ship, leaving a shocked stillness in her wake.

The next day, Ingel Stroebel announced the German group was moving to their land claim, the Minen, in the far northwest, located south of the Black Forest and west of the Lower Helades. Not to be outdone, Bain Macnab announced the Scotts were also moving to the far north in the western area just beyond the Dark Forest and the impassible Helades, where many caves dotted the landscape.

Emboldened, the Basques and Spaniards jumped in, the Basques moving to the northern Rolando Hills, where many coves and bays lined the western coast. The Spaniards jumped onboard with their move to the southern Rolando Hills and across the Land River. By default, the English group continued to occupy the Southern Grasslands, where their new crops thrived, hinting at a bountiful harvest come fall.

The separation required adjustments. XO Koralsky

gave each group a shuttle and permission to use the Hawker for refueling. However, once the Hawker's fuel ran out, these shuttles would be grounded and useless.

She ordered, "So, gentlemen, reserve the shuttles for emergency flights down here."

Hans divided up the salvaged and cut up aluminum pieces, from which they made many wheeled carts. They also made arrow heads and spear points giving each group potential ways to hunt. Raven divided the copper cups, plates, and bowls made from the native copper vein, along with substantial food reserves from the ship.

The English group gave each of the departing groups a dozen chickens and a rooster, along with breeding instructions. Likewise, the Spaniards gave each group a dozen horses, including one stud. Begrudgingly, the Basques gave each group five cows, one milk cow, and a bull. Finally, the Scotts gave each group a half dozen sheep.

With each individual toting what they could, the German group left first, heading northeast. After leaving a breeding pair of border collies with the English group, the Scottish departed to barking and baying, their shepherds and dogs leading the sheep and goats ahead of the main party.

Once that pile of confusion vanished, the Basques and their herd of cattle headed out. Many of their cattle carried crude packs, leading Zigor to say they migrated in style. Still, they had a long journey ahead. But with food sources so plentiful, no one worried about the length of the trip. The Spanish group waited until the next day before getting organized and leaving.

The four groups' overall plans had their shuttle flying ahead, preparing their best choice for their new town. XO Koralsky sent along a portable, hand-cranked comm set they could use to get in touch with the ship, as long as the ship survived.

As they watched the horsemen disappearing over the horizon, Raven said, "I'm really worried about them. How will they survive out there? We're halfway through a year here. Winters are likely to be nasty. They've no food stores nor homes built yet. Why couldn't they just stay through winter? Put their differences on hold for once."

Adrian Reiner didn't go with his fellow Germans, choosing instead to stay with Julie. He said, "Their antagonism runs deep. Honestly, they are the last holdouts of our people, who refused to immigrate or populate new worlds for the Sol Empire. Here, they wanted to make sure no one barged in on their mining claims. So foolish. What good will gold do them here? And moving without knowing what winters will be like or food stores or living quarters—they're all being stupid. They should have wintered over here, using these months to gather food supplies and build homes and a million other things. Heck, I think there might be iron ores to the east of here where the Lower Helades joins the Southern Grasslands."

"Really?" Raven asked.

"Yeah. Julie and I've been mapping gravity abnormalities recorded during shuttle flights. We think there's a substantial deposit there, but it could also be gold or lead or other heavier minerals."

"Take our shuttle and check it out. We could really use an iron mine of our own," Raven said.

"Great. Except I can't fly it. Don't know how."

Hans, overhearing them, said, "I'll take him. I really need to get out of this ship, even if it's just for a day."

"Hey, that's not a bad idea. I'll tag along, if you guys don't mind. Bit of fresh air and sightseeing," Raven said.

An hour later, Adrian said, "The gravity abnormalities are registering now. It goes from here eastward for fifty miles, we estimate. North-south, it averages about twenty miles wide. Guess you'll have to land."

"On it," Hans said. "Dig out those new shovels I made."

Shovels in hand, they exited the shuttle, the ground upthrust they stood on, apparent. The grasslands gave way to a rockier ground. Adrian and Raven collected rock samples, while Hans poked around with a shovel.

"If I'm not mistaken, this is iron ore," he said, "but looks like it contains traces of tin ore, maybe."

"Isn't this a gold nugget?" Raven asked, showing the pair what she'd found.

"Aye, it's soft, not like fool's gold, which is hard. Collect more and you'll be rich," Hans said.

Raven laughed. "And what will a sack of this buy me here?"

"Minor detail," Hans said, grinning.

"We can make golden goblets to trade with the Germans," Adrian said.

"Over here," Hans said, having shoveled loose soil off the underlying upthrust rock. "Definitely ores. Iron, I'd say here, but with some tin off to one side and lead off to the other. Strange combination."

Later, they flew eastward, sampling another section of land, finding more of the same but with the addition of a thin vein of gold catching the yellow sunlight.

By the time the yellow noon passed, the sun illuminated the eastern remnants of the Lower Helades. But the black color caught their attention. Hans insisted on flying there to "check it out."

After landing and walking up to the beginning of the black ground, Hans said, "Well, this we can use. That's an exposed coal vein! With these resources, we can make our own steel or ironworks. And maybe have heat for our houses. We'll need to get a mining operation here."

"Do any of us know how to mine? Smelter? Or work iron?" Raven asked.

"Not exactly, but the computer can educate us. We'll need wagons to haul ore and coal back to the ship. Lots to do. Lots," Hans said, grinning like a little kid in a candy store.

When they returned, Faith's muscles eased. "Now, we won't depend upon those Stroebels. Any way we can use the coal to heat our homes instead of all this chopping wood? I've got blisters from helping cut up firewood while you were gone."

"Yes, as long as we have a solid grate. Maybe I can

make some from parts from the ship," Hans said. "I can't believe we're having to reinvent everything. We need pickaxes and wagons and work horses."

Faith said, "Take it one step at a time. We have a few horses, so we need digging tools and wagons. Focus on making those. Then, we'll assign an expedition to dig up some coal and ores. After that, we'll worry about how to use them."

"How do we make wheels for the wagons?" Raven asked. "Figure a box would do for the wagon bed. Wooden axles, perhaps? Gods, we're reinventing the wheel!"

That cracked the others up. When the laughter died down, Faith said, "Yep, reinventing ourselves, too."

"Ah, there you are, Raven. Could you take a look at my budding castle? Something's not right with it," Ace said.

She and Faith followed Faith's boyfriend to the upthrust and the new rock quarry. Already, Ace had carved out many rectangular blocks so heavy that only the personal lifter device they used to handle loading heavy loads into the cruiser's cargo hold could lift these blocks. He had constructed three walls about six feet tall.

"It's not stable. What am I doing wrong?"

Raven looked the construction over and said, "Buttresses. You need to buttress the walls, perhaps every twenty feet. The corners serve that purpose here, but not on those longer runs. It's looking good. How tall are you planning to go?"

"The ship's crane can lift them up about twenty-five feet, so I'm shooting for a complete second floor. Not sure of the roof yet. Cathedral vaulted ceilings look impressive, but I've yet to figure out how they made them. Those are going to be the fireplaces. Each suite will have its own fireplace. I'm gambling winters are frigid here, so we'll need heat all the time. The thick walls will provide insulation to retain the heat."

"Will it be done by winter?" Faith asked.

"Dunno. So damn much to do. With luck, the suites on the ground floor will be. I don't relish living in the ship any longer than necessary."

Chapter 12 Between Work and Inventions

With good news to share, Raven called a meeting.

"There are five hundred twenty of us and plenty of work to go around if we're to survive winter. Thanks to Julie and Adrian, we have our own iron ore, tin, and lead. Even better, we've a vein of coal waiting for mining. Plus, many of you have seen Ace's castle. He hopes to have it completed by winter, or at least ready for partial occupation.

"So now we have much to do and perhaps five months to complete them. We need someone to work these new mines. Specifically, the coal and iron ore veins. We need wagons constructed, which means also we need wagon wheels invented. If we have the right collars, we can pull the ore back with the horses. Pots. With harvest coming later on, we need lots of pottery to store our produce and seeds for next year. We must put up many cords of wood to stay warm and to fire the clay and so on. And there is the daily chore of finding food for our tables.

"Thanks to Lyn Norton who has made four duplicate copies of the Basque beehive, I can announce some bees have taken up residence. Honey for our future needs. Sabrina Baker wants us to make an oven she can use to bake bread and other items for us, assuming we can invent ways to harvest the wheat crop which is thriving. Come up with a way to make a mill to grind our wheat into flower. We need wooden water buckets invented, along with rope. We need to learn to spin wool into cloth to make warmer clothes before winter comes.

"We need to invent paper and pens so we can make books to use to teach our children. Once the few computers we're using now die, how will we be able to pass on our knowledge? How will we be able to teach our children how to read and write? How to do math? We need ways to pass on our advanced knowledge, which our children's children won't have if we can't do these things before it's too late.

"Faith has been scrounging up all reserve apparel items along with unneeded blankets and cloths such as rags and towels, which we can convert into clothing somehow. We need wash tubs designed so we can wash our clothes. And looms. We need to invent weaving looms so we can make rugs and blankets and bolts of cloth."

Someone called out, "And babies! We need lots more children if we're to survive, isn't that right?"

"Yes, we've done the calculations. She's right. If our people are to have a future and not die off in a generation or two, our calculations suggest women of childbearing age need to have four children. Next generation, they only need three. If so, our group should be able to thrive and grow. We must expand. Never stay the same or contract. That's a death sentence. Some of you already have one or two children, which is excellent. But all of us who can need to have more babies."

"What about you? What about XO Koralsky?" the woman called out again.

"I think all of us who can should hold off on getting pregnant until we get ourselves through the coming winter. There's so darn much work that must be done and we don't know how long the good weather will hold.

"Another thing about having babies. We've a very limited gene pool. To avoid having malformed children in the future, the fathers of the proposed four children per woman should be different. I know some of you married couples might object to this, but think of it as a safety measure for your grandchildren. If we don't, their children could well be malformed. If you know your history, that's what happened to the Hapsburg dynasty and the Egyptian dynasties.

"But that isn't to say you should break up your marriages and families. Rather, just accept that some of your children's fathers might not be your husband's offspring and that your husband could father other women's children. Above all, we want to raise our children with strong family values, which stranded on this remote world is more vital than ever."

"Hey, what about lesbians?" Poppy Miller asked.

"I'm not asking all women to marry men. Rather, I'm asking you to have babies and raise them as your families. If you don't want males living with you, that's fine. But creating enough children in this next generation is vital for everyone. But we will not stand for rapes. Guys, just ask her and honor her wishes if she says no. Perhaps it should be ladies' picks. We'll vote on that detail later."

That brought cheers from some women.

"I'll be making up a master list of these things we need. Then, I'll visit with each one of you. Together, we'll assign you one of these tasks, one you'd like to attempt. Working together, I believe we can do these things, given enough time and will power. What we do with the rest of our lives will set the pattern for the lives of our grandchildren and their children. Keep them in mind when the tasks we face seem too harsh, too impossible. For what we do in the next few years will have an enormous impact on their lives."

After the meeting broke up and people resumed their chores, Faith said, "I can see why these people elected you to be their liaison and spokesperson. You've told them what needs to be done and gave them reasons to haul ass doing it. You're good, Raven Cooper, damn good."

"Thanks. So much to do. So little time and resources."

Raven then walked over to inspect Ace's castle. "How's the buttresses coming along?"

"Don't know why I didn't think of them, Raven. As you can see, I've got one already installed. Made the wall extremely solid. I bet we can go for three or four stories now."

Raven laughed. "But you'll have to build cranes to lift the blocks that high. I'll be satisfied if we have a place to winter over."

"I'm making sure every suite has a good chimney,

what with coal as our fuel. It burns hotter, so I'm adjusting the fireplace walls accordingly. Say, you are friends with Faith. Can I ask you something?"

"Sure."

"I thought she and I were lovers, going to get hitched one day and raise a family. We've even had sex twice, even though that's hard to do on the ship. So little privacy. But now that we are free of that constraint, she seems to have gotten cold towards me. Has she said anything about me to you?"

"She said you are her boyfriend, Ace. She still thinks of you that way. Not every woman enjoys intercourse. I found it most unpleasant and messy. Doesn't mean I won't do my part and try to have four children. That's critical for the long-term survival of our people. It's not that I don't dislike men either. I couldn't do what you're doing for us. Building the castle. I do like you, Ace. It's just I've never had any pleasure from a guy poking it in me. I know I'm weird that way. I think Faith is that way too, at least somewhat. Give her time to adjust. She's lost her XO position and the authority she's used to having."

"Ah, that's gotta be it. She always strove to be the best. She had her sights set on becoming a commander of her own cruiser, and she promised when she got that promotion, she'd insist I become her pilot. Now all of that, her childhood dreams, are smashed. No wonder she's been rather cold to me of late."

"Give her time and space, Ace. That's what all of us need right now."

"Thanks. I feel tons better now. Back to work for me. Got a castle to build."

Back at her computer onboard the ship, Raven worked up the list of needed jobs and inventions. After printing it off, she resolved to visit each person and get their names beside an item on the list.

Faith dropped by. "Saw you talking to Ace this morning. What's he want?"

"Wanted to know what you felt about him." She relayed what they'd discussed.

"Thanks, Raven. I am very lost about now. Ever since I saw a spaceship model when I was four, I wanted to command a fighting ship. Worked my ass off to be the best and made it to XO. Now I feel like a fish out of water."

"I know. You've lost your lifelong goal and purpose. So many of us have. I was all set to begin teaching physics to teens when the fall term began on New Terra. I'm still going to do that, only I have to get us surviving and a school built. Then, I can finally do what I wanted to do. Share my love of how things work.

"But in your case, Faith, you must come up with a new purpose, a new goal to achieve. I know you're overseeing the cannibalization of your ship. But once that's done, then what?"

"Exactly, Raven. Then what? I'm trained to be a commander of a fighting spaceship. That's all I know."

"Look over this long list. Is there something on this that pricks your interest even a little?"

After a long, serious pause, Faith sighed. "No, not really. I like to make sure others are getting their jobs done."

"Ah, ha. I'm adding a new item to the list. With all these actions going on and at nearly the same time, I'm going to need an overseer to do just that. Someone to organize and direct these actions. To see to it they get finished. That's your new job, Faith. Job Coordinator."

"Hey, I like that. It's what I know how to do and enjoy doing. I feel like I've just lost twenty pounds. Wow! You know, that's been worrying me since we landed. What will I do now?"

"Okay. I'm off to get a good fit for the other five hundred and seventeen people."

"Better you than me. You are a natural at this, Raven. You're the sexiest woman here."

"Except I haven't experienced any pleasure from sex."

"What? Well, honestly, I don't enjoy it when Ace fucks me, either. I sense how much he needs that form of intimacy, but I sure don't. I think only a woman knows how to make another woman relish what her body offers. Maybe someday we can try, Raven. I'd love to sleep with you. In my eyes, you're the hottest woman on this planet."

Raven flushed.

"But I best let you tackle all the others. I can't tell you how relieved I feel knowing what my new position will be once I see to the cannibalization of the Hawker."

A week passed before Raven had visited each person. With everyone, she got to know them a little first and helped them pick the "right" activity that best suited them. Even the children wanted tasks to do, though Raven insisted they continue their education via the computer system's educational programs.

One young teen wanted to help, even though she was still in high school. "Look, everyone else is working, helping us all survive. I want to help too, besides doing all this book learning."

"What do you really enjoy doing?"

"That's just it. I wanted to be a chef at a five-star restaurant. That's not gonna happen now, it is? Haven't seen any restaurants around here, have you?"

"Nope. What I wouldn't give for some French fries," Raven said, bringing agreement from the teen. "What about taking time out of your studies each day around noon to make and deliver sandwiches to the workers? That way, they don't have to stop what they're doing and come back to the ship and make themselves a lunch."

"Can I do that? Really?"

Watching her eyes light up with a new valuable purpose beyond studying convinced Raven she was doing the right actions.

Chapter 13 Progress

A week later, a team headed off to begin mining operations. One man Jerry-rigged up two wagons from wheels from devices on the ship along with logs and wicker weaving for the sides. Another woman created a yoke and harness for two horses to pull the contraptions. One carried the dozen people and their gear while the other would carry back ores they dug. As they set off, hundreds cheered them on. Raven made sure everyone could watch them leave. Anything to keep morale up.

Another pottery woman worked out very flat pieces and used a stylus of aluminum to etch the basic math tables and the alphabet on it. Then she fired it and showed Raven.

"It's not much of a textbook, but we can have letters and math notes on these clay tablets. The kids could then have fresh clay tablets to practice their writing or do math problems on it. When done, since they haven't been fired, they could be smoothed and reused. It's a start."

"Brilliant. If we can't make paper, this will definitely work. We'll need quite a lot of tablets to contain what students must know. Go ahead. Make a dozen alphabet tablets and basic math tables. We can use them for the beginning students, no matter what."

Adrian and Julie made an extensive survey of the entire Southern Grasslands, from the Land River just west of the Three Peaks all the way east to the coast just over the Lower Helades and from the South Fork northward to the Middle Fork. They mapped out many woodland patches and a hundred other resources that could be used. In fact, they discovered several smaller lakes, teaming with fish. And where the South Fork merged into the Land River, they identified a vast patch of marshland with many kinds of reeds.

A week later, some women harvested reeds, forming

them into much needed baskets. For the next month, they continued making forays to cut and use the reeds.

A month later, the first load of ores arrived, half coal, half iron ore. The drivers returned just as soon as they unloaded their wagon. Next, Raven had those who wanted to learn to make steel or iron tools begin smelter operations, following the computer's suggested information on how to do it. In case of fire, she had them set up their operations away from the ship, new homes, and the inhabited zones around them.

Another month later, the men displayed the first iron axes and knives made, along with the new blacksmith anvil. Again, Raven wanted all five hundred twenty to witness each of these successes, building hope and morale.

Another dozen who liked to fish spent their days fishing in the river. After gutting them with the new aluminum knives, they spitted the filets and allowed them to dry for the winter.

When harvest time came, half the population shared in the lengthy work. They cut wheat, barley, and oats. Some experimentation yielded the best way to knock the kernels off the shafts. They took care to keep the grains dry, setting aside enough to provide seed for next year's crop. Raven insisted they set aside twenty-five percent more than they had planted this year, in case not all germinated. Workers bundled the shafts together with reed ties and stored them in the ship's cargo hold to feed the few animals they had.

The potatoes, sweet potatoes, and carrots thrived in this soil. Again, they stored the produce in the new reed baskets or new clay pottery. Beans, lima beans, and peas ended up being stored in clay pots as well.

Later, men took turns sheering the few sheep they had, saving the precious wool. Women who wanted to learn to create thread, carded and spun the fibers into spools. Others had already created two experimental looms, using available pieces of string from the ship. Quickly, they worked out how to make the first bolts of wool cloth. They promised to spend all winter making more looms and more bolts of cloth.

Again, Raven insisted everyone look at these final products being produced. Anything to keep up morale.

As the high temperatures cooled, the beekeepers harvested some of the honey, again storing it in smaller clay pots others had made. That's when a key discovery happened.

Beekeeper Miller showed Raven the evidence he'd uncovered. "See the remains of those yellow buttercup-like flowers that are all over the grasslands? Well, the bees love them. Look there. That's where all this fine white dust over everything comes from. These plants. The bees are covered in the white stuff."

Raven summoned Doctors Kelly Johnson and Marshall Wu, showing them the origin of the mysterious white organic phosphorous. She said, "I hope it's not harmful because those yellow flowers grow all over the grasslands. No eluding it."

"Well, so far it seems harmless," Marshall said, "but we're still keeping a close eye on everyone's health. Things like cancer or TB or any number if ailments can happen if our bodies reject this organic compound. But you're right. If it's harmful to us, we can't avoid it."

In addition, three women had their babies during these months, two girls and a boy. Raven had the proud parents show off their babies to the entire group.

She said, "Let's welcome the first newborns to our new world, Landfall. And does anyone have a stash of diapers or baby clothes they could donate? I can see we need to plan for this, too."

That brought a round of chuckles and smiles. "See, I can't think of everything."

Someone yelled back. "Yeah, but you've done a damn good job of it!"

While Raven smiled, others clapped. However, she knew soon she'd have to ask the women to get pregnant, including herself. She held off because winter hadn't arrived.

Fall brought a distinct change in the weather. Days

of freezing rain happened with alarming frequency. Still, iron ore and coal continued to arrive, stored temporarily in the cargo hold. Others prepared winter quarters in other parts of the hold for the many animals, though they continued using all the eggs the chickens produced each day.

"Come look at this!" Faith called out to Raven. "Migrating birds. Sort of like ducks, don't you think?"

"I bet they're wintering over on the southern coast below the South Fork. One day, we'll have to check out that coast," Raven said. "I bet they summer up in the northern Lake District. I wonder if they're good to eat?"

"Speaking of that, besides the fish, we've very little protein laid in for the winter," Faith said. "Now that we have more sharp tools, we could butcher one caribou and see if it's fit to eat. And those rabbit-like furry things, too."

"Good point. I'll leave that to you. Make use of your armory for now. If it pans out, we'll have to work out ways to kill them with arrows or spears or something. Our grandchildren won't have blasters to use."

"Or the few antique guns, for that matter. On it, Boss."

Raven smiled at the reference and watched Faith walk away with a noticeable bounce in her step.

Tye Tucker had Raven come see his latest creation. "It's a grain grinder. We need to make flower, because I'm not giving up bread. I found two stones that are pretty flat. Had Ace help me get them smooth. Built this contraption."

"Are those gears?" Raven asked.

"Yes, wooden gears. We can hook two horses here or four men. We walk around in the circle, turning that shaft which, via the gears, turns the top stone. A piece of paper is all that can fit between the stones. This lever raises the top stone so you can spread more wheat kernels to be ground."

His wife, Sabrina, said, "This is what it produces." She held up a small pot with the first of the ground flower. "Now we can make bread."

Raven had everyone come by during the day to see

this latest miracle invention, again raising the group's morale.

But try as he might, Ace didn't have the castle ready for occupation before the weather became too cold, icy, and snowy for him to continue. After packing up his equipment for the winter, storing them inside the half-built stone building, he lent a hand to those cutting and bringing in the last of the tall grasses as fodder for the cows and horses. Until the weather turned too bad to be outdoors, he helped where he could, as did many others, whose primary jobs took a winter hiatus.

By now, Hans had cannibalized the stern section of the ship near the ion engines. Here, sections were exposed to the elements and thus bulkhead doors sealed them from the rest of the ship. The nuclear power generator continued to run life support, including providing heat throughout the ship. Hans had already blocked off the heating ducts to the exposed sections. Further, since the ship now provided support to only five hundred and not the original two thousand five hundred, he also blocked off major sections of the living quarters.

His goal: make the power plant last as long as possible. Besides providing heat and light, it also recharged disintegrators and a myriad of other power tools. Once the nuclear fuel ran out, manual generators could provide some electricity until the ion engines fuel ran out. Since they now had only one shuttle, that fuel consumption had slowed way down. For Hans, the big worry was how much would the winter tax the nuclear power plant? Could it even supply enough internal heat to offset the expected cold? He didn't relay his concerns to anyone, though.

Before the onset of winter, a rider leading another horse arrived from the northeast. Jurgen Klein came to trade.

"I've brought a horse-load of nuts. We've an overabundance of nut trees up in Meinen. Herr Stroebel wishes to trade these for whatever your garden produced that you can spare."

Raven tasted a nut and agreed to the swap. She said, "We should establish trade between our lands. Once we can produce reliable wagons, we can trade far more than you can carry in your saddlebags. How are you fixed for the winter?"

"We've built a dozen large extended family homes. We should be okay if the food holds out. Like you, we've put up a lot of dried fish. We've also captured a dozen caribou. It seems they are docile enough to be trained to carry packs and riders. If our survival depends on it, we'll butcher some. They taste gamey, though."

Not long after he left, Miguel Perez rode in from the west. The Spaniard came to trade for garden produce as well, offering a stud horse. Raven accepted, knowing that we needed more horses than the original six and that ours were mares.

For days after that, Raven expected to hear from the Basques or Scotts, but by now the weather had become too unpredictable, far too risky to travel overland. But the other two didn't send their shuttles down.

XO Koralsky kept in contact with the four groups via the hand-cranked communication sets, whose weak signals could be picked up by the ship's powerful receiver. Their monthly calls kept her appraised of their survival attempts. The Scotts promised a load of wool come spring.

Chapter 14 First Winter

The yellow sun became noticeably smaller in the noon sky. The wild weather swings when the red sun stopped being visible when the yellow sun was up became even wilder. At first, sheets of freezing rain blown by gale force winds prevented any outside access as they huddled inside the ship. Ace, of course, made more plans to strengthen up his castle, come spring.

The sheets gave way to blinding snowstorms. Yet once both suns became visible at the same time, the powerful winds subsided. But the snow did not.

"Isn't it ever going to stop snowing?" Faith asked, gazing out an observation window on the bridge.

Ace grimaced. "We suspected winters would be bad, but this is ridiculous. I may have to double the castle wall's thickness to withstand this level of cold. Hans says it's ice cubes down in the blocked off cargo hold areas. It's a wonder the ship can keep us warm enough. He said heaters are going full blast. But I wonder how severe this is draining the power packs. We'll freeze to death if we have a power failure."

"We're going to have to lay in hundreds of cords to heat homes or cart back tons of coal," Faith said. "I hope the other four groups can survive this. Were they prepared enough?"

"Somehow, we really, really need to make tons of warm clothing," Raven said, shivering. "I can't seem to warm up enough. Dreary London was never like this."

"I think it was pretty miserable up in cold Scotland, so our Scotts group is probably used to this. Maybe."

"I bet the Basques and Spaniards are the most at risk," Raven said. "Their native climate was never this bad. At least I don't think it was. Have we heard from them?"

Faith checked her crude calendar she'd taped beside the comm set. She'd marked out each month with its twenty days, which was Landfall's year or time for one revolution around the red sun. The year consisted of twenty of these months, all blocked out on her wall. She expected one of the other four groups to call in on each of the four five-day weeks. Week One, the Germans would call. And so on down the line.

She'd rigged up an alarm system to alert her of the incoming call so that she didn't have to sit around all hours of the day during the week of the expected touching-base call. Thus far, the system had worked well. But the worse the weather became, the more she worried about the other groups.

"Why couldn't they have listened to Raven's wise words and winter here on the ship before heading off to their land claims?" she asked Ace.

"Greed," he said, ending her speculation.

"It's a total whiteout outside. Can't see anything through my window."

"Glad I'm not trying to fly in this."

"What are we going to do if one group calls in an emergency?"

"Shuttles can't fly in this. They're stuck wherever they're at. We couldn't get to them by air. Foot travel is impossible. Hell, I can't even see the two houses we built or the sides of my castle. If you donned your spacesuit, perhaps you could be outside—temperature wise. Couldn't see where you're going, though."

Faith sighed. "I know. Raven pleaded with them and suggested winters might make travel impossible. The idiots. Are all men foolish idiots?"

"Hope you aren't including me or Hans or Adrian in that."

Her eyes met his. "No, you're right. I'm so pessimistic right now. There's nothing I can actually do right now. Bored stiff. Everything's at a standstill."

"And will be for months. We should have brought along some puzzles. Maybe a card game. Think Raven's up for one?"

The two doctors dropped by to visit with Raven,

suggesting perhaps the time had come to begin making the desired number of babies. Dr. Wu said, "Here, the gestation period will be 13.5 months. So getting pregnant now will allow the baby to be born during the summer months."

"Is it wise to have so many women pregnant simultaneously?" Raven asked.

"Between us? No. Perhaps limit it to twenty-five for this first try."

"Okay, I'll make the announcement and get the details worked out."

Over the ship-wide intercom, Raven made the announcement. "So our doctors want to limit the number of babies being born this summer. They've decided we should limit it to twenty-five pregnancies this time. Any of you who are already pregnant, let me know right away. It's my job to coordinate this. And I will take volunteers who want to have a baby this summer. The first step is to get a thorough checkup before you make the attempt. Our doctors assured me that if all goes well, then we can work out a way to stagger due dates so we don't overload our doctors.

"Also, those of you who have suggested you'd like to learn to be a doctor or to learn how to be a midwife, contact Dr. Marshal Wu or Dr. Kelly Johnson. Now's the time to begin your training. If they accept you, let me know so I can mark it on the log. Thank you."

Ace said, "So, Faith, have you decided now is the time for us to have a child? You know I really want kids."

Faith looked at Raven, who looked back and spoke up.

"Not all women relish sexual intercourse. I certainly didn't like it, which is why I'm still unattached. Faith is the same way, I think. However, you're right. We need to do our part, just as all other women who can must do."

"Look, we don't have to do it every night. I'm in love with you, Faith, or rather, I was. But I've realized that was because you were my XO. A climb the ladder thing. Now I like to think I've matured, changed. For the better. I count you both as my very best friends. We're supposed to have lots of children, and I want to share in that, too. And if Raven's right and each child should have a different father, well, I'm okay with that too. As long as I can help raise them. Besides, there's no way officially to get married, now that the Commander is dead. There's not a priest among our group."

Raven sighed before replying. "Okay, I should be one of the first to get pregnant. After all, it's my data that I'm depending on for our population survival calculations. I'm okay with you being the father, Ace, and you can have the role of the baby's father, too. We're going to need male support raising such large families."

"If she's willing, then so am I, Ace," Raven said. "She has a strong point. We'll need you to step up and be the father to the two of us, even if we end up with three other men's children. Kids need a strong father just as much as they need powerful mothers."

"Woo hoo! You two have just made me the happiest man on Landfall! You can count on me to be there. Always."

"Even at three in the morning with smelly diapers and crying babies?" Faith asked.

"It comes with fatherhood," he said, determinedly.

Raven said, "If we do this, Ace, there's no backing out of it."

"Go get your checkups, and tell me when it's the right time," Ace said, glee in his eyes.

The two women reported to Dr. Wu and Dr. Johnson. Dr. Wu said, "First thing is a complete physical checkup, including CAT scans. I'll take Raven for her scan while you handle Faith's checkup."

An hour later, Dr. Wu studied the head scan of Raven's.

Puzzled, she asked, "Is something wrong? I know I've been having dull headaches for weeks. Tumor?"

"No, nothing like that. It's your pituitary gland, that small, pea-sized endocrine gland there. Only it's no longer pea-sized. Try quarter-sized. It's grown some, which probably accounts for those dull headaches."

"What's it do?"

"Got time for a medical lesson? Its primary function is to produce and release several hormones that help carry out important bodily functions responsible for your growth, your metabolism, aids in reproduction, helps your body handle stress or trauma, keeps your water and salt balanced. It's like the body's thermostat, sending signals to cause your body to heat or cool. It does this by releasing hormones.

"Don't worry. You are healthy. It's just I would like to work out why this gland only is growing in size. I'll keep you posted. Now go change places with Faith, please."

A few minutes later, Dr. Johnson began asking his questions while taking her vitals.

"Seems my pituitary thing has doubled in size," Raven said. "We think that might be why I've had some dull head pains."

"How interesting. We've seen three others whose pituitary gland has grown. This isn't normal, but so far, we've detected no side effects of its growth. You haven't had periods of feeling overly cold or overheated?"

She shook her head.

"Well, if you do, come see us at once. Honestly, you and Faith are in very good condition. Nothing to worry about. You have our okay to have a baby in the summer. Have you worked out how you can have four different fathers?"

"Yeah, doc. The woman gets to ask each man she wants to father her next baby."

"Ah, lady's choice. I like that. Should go over well."

Later, when they returned to the bridge, Ace asked, "Well? All okay?"

Faith said, "Yes. Perfect health. So I guess I can't put this off any longer. But later. Tonight, perhaps."

With their checkups done, Raven and Faith shared a cup of hot tea.

"Don't know when we'll ever have a brew like this

again, once we use up the last tea bags," Faith said. "But it looks like we'll have to use Ace's stud services now. It's so unpleasant, though. Sex, I mean."

"And messy. I didn't get aroused, so it was painful," Raven said.

"Same here. Ace is handsome, and you can't find a nicer guy, but..."

"Yeah, I know. Doesn't arouse you. Or me, for that matter."

"But you do," Faith said. "Arouse me." She flushed and became quiet.

A thoughtful look covered Raven's face. She said, "What if I aroused you first? When you're hot, let him do his thing. Avoid the problem."

"Would you? God, that would help. Plus, I'm insisting I be on top, doing him," Faith said. "If it works, I'll do the same for you. Maybe we can make this work. Lord knows, we have to have children."

"Should be easy to pull off, since we're sharing the same cabin now. We've shut down as much of the ship as possible to stretch that nuclear power plant's lifetime."

That night as Raven caressed Faith's naked body, she had her first hint something in her had changed. She sensed what Faith's body needed to get acutely aroused. Then she slipped into the tiny bathroom, ushering Ace out. Thank heavens for a tiny nightlight, she thought. A few minutes later, she heard Ace departing, and she slipped back into the cabin proper.

Faith whispered, "Thanks. That really worked perfectly. Now comes the messy part. Wait. What're we going to do when the tampon supply is gone?"

"Things just got even messier for us women," Raven said.

The next night, they reversed rolls. For the first time, Raven had a mostly pleasureful experience.

Meanwhile, the howling winds continued to rage. Snow now covered the western side of the ship, and the temperature plummeted during the nights when no suns traversed the sky. Other times, when only the red sun graced the nighttime skies, the temperatures moderated. At these times, snow and ice began to melt a little.

The other groups kept touch during the worst of the winter. The Scotts and Germans survived the worst by hunkering down in their cave systems and burning cords of wood, while the Basques had settled in a sheltered cove surrounded by taller hills, which protected them from the harshest weather. Right on the coast, the winds across the waters moderated the frigid temperatures felt inland. Their big complaint was fish. They grew tired of eating so much fish.

The Spanish group who settled in the southern Rolando Hills also stayed close to the ocean shores and benefitted from the water's moderating effects. Still, three members died from the cold, and by spring, many were starving, desperate for food assistance. Zigor flew two cows down to them, which provided some critical meat.

If nothing else, the other four groups realized following Raven's advice would have been a far wiser choice.

A month later, Raven noticed the yellow sun had grown larger in the sky, announcing the coming of spring. When the group members finally could venture outside the ship, many thanked Raven for all she'd done to keep them alive. Some claimed she was a goddess.

Now that her morning sickness had passed, Raven sensed the new life growing within her. Relaxing before work one morning, she slipped into what she later called a vision.

Her body felt old, very old, though she could only see her wrinkled hands as she lay in bed in her suite in Cooper Castle, as they called Ace's creation. Five stories tall, the many suites could house two thousand, though some weren't yet occupied. An attached stable housed their every-growing herd of horses. She heard the first of five wagons pulling out, heading for their eastern mines. Then, her four children knocked and entered. One threw open the heavy drapes, one stoked the coal fire, and one helped her sit up.

The fourth said, "Brought you breakfast, Mom. How are you feeling today? Toby had her second boy last night. We didn't want to wake you. You've now got an even dozen grandchildren and three great-grandchildren. Not bad, eh? We expect the emissaries will arrive late morning. Ben's been tracking their progress with his eagles. We've accomplished so much, Mom, all due to you. The Cooper Celebration will begin at noon, when the emissaries are here to join in celebrating what you've brought to us all."

"Hey, you okay?" Faith's voice disturbed the vision. The stark aluminum walls of the tiny spaceship's cabin came into focus.

"Think so. Had a sort of vision. Of the future. Maybe it's just pregnancy hormones."

"Tell me about them! I still can't eat breakfast. Good visions, I hope."

Raven smiled. "Well, it's time to get to work. We've a zillion things to get done before the next winter."

"Don't remind me. Well, guess you have. Hans revised his estimates. There is a slim chance the nuclear power plant will get us through a second winter. But he doesn't want us to count on it."

Chapter 15 Growth

Raven looked at her voluminous planning pages. Winter has its uses. Time to plan. Let's see what I should press forward today.

Ace said, "I'm off to the castle. Can I take ten men with me? If that power plant gives out, we'll need the castle operational."

"Yes, take your usual work crew. That's all I can spare right now. The rest need to work on plowing and getting the spring crops in."

Raven visited Scarlet Riggs, who oversaw the garden project last year. "Hi, when you plan this year's garden, I want you to double its size."

"That's just what I was going to say. Funny. Anyway, I want to move the tuber plots to where we had the oats last year. I think the ground there will produce a much better crop. It's funny. Now I'm having dreams about my crops."

"Good ones, I hope. Yes, use your own judgment on that. I'll get some hands to help clear more land."

"More crops mean more food and more that we can trade with others for things we need. Like wool. We're going to need much warmer clothing," Scarlet said.

Raven smiled. "Great minds think alike." She left Scarlet feeling quite pleased that her suggestions were readily accepted.

Dusty Baker caught her attention. "Raven, we're going to need much better chicken coops and places where they can roost and hatch eggs. Especially in the winter. I've had some visionary ideas about how we can do this, if you want to hear them."

"Interesting. Yes, we might not have survived if it weren't for the zillions of eggs your flocks produced last year."

"Well, rumors have it that Ace's castle will be ready

for occupation this fall. I want to build a chicken house as an add-on to his facility. That way, we can keep them warm in the winter, handle their needs, and collect eggs without going outside. I couldn't imagine how we could have gone outside the spaceship last winter. Bitter cold. Deep snow. No vision. You'd get lost in a minute out there. So I want a better way. Besides, rumor has it the power pack might not last another winter. That true?"

"Yes, Hans has worries we might run out during the next winter. He's got a fuel backup generator system for that eventuality. But I'm hoping we can move out of the ship for this winter. So go coordinate your plans with Ace. Tell him if he needs more workers, to let me know how many."

"Oh, thank you so much, Raven, for believing me and my silly visions."

"Visions aren't silly, Dusty. Keep those chickens healthy and producing. Excellent plans you have."

She dashed off to see Ace at the castle construction site as Shepherd Smith walked up.

"Excuse me, Miss Cooper. Can I have a word with you?"

"Sure, anytime. Raven, just Raven."

He smiled. "Raven. I've had this crazy idea—a vision is more like it—all winter long. We need a sawmill. A way to turn these tree logs into boards for building."

"No kidding. It's a priority on my list for this year."

"Well, I think I know a way to make it work. It came to me in a sort of vision. How to make a cutting blade move at very high speeds. That's the key. Right now, the guys are using crude aluminum chopping tools to peel layers off to make a crude board. I looked up sawmills to see how it's done. Motors drive very high-speed blades which tear through logs as they push them past the whirling blades. Our problem is we don't have those motors, nor will we ever have them. So in my vision, a combination of gears can take something moving slowly and output something moving fast.

"I'd like the chance to see if I can make it work.

Inspired by the miller machine last year. In my vision, it should work using simple horse power, like the miller uses. Uses wooden gears for now, until we can make steel gears."

"If you can make real boards, everyone will love you! That's something we need ASAP. Do you need help constructing it?"

"Well, yes. A couple of people who can work with wood, if you can spare them. I know there's so much we gotta do. Rumor has it the power pack might die by winter."

"Okay, I'll send a couple your way. Make it work, please."

Later Lyn Norton called on Raven. She said, "I'd like your permission to make more beehives. The four duplicate copies of the Basque beehive are filling up with bees this year. I had a vision that we could easily quadruple our honey supply, if only I could make more hives."

"Love that vision. Yes, your honey has been a bit hit. What do you need to make your vision come true?"

"If someone could cut down a tree for me, I can work on cutting it into the crude boards I need. Hans thinks he has some spare grills I can use on the insides."

"Excellent. Just keep the hives away from habitation sites. We don't want to get stung. I'll round up someone for you today. If we get enough honey made each year, we can barter with it to the other groups."

"Funny, but that's kind of how I saw it in my vision. Us trading honey pots for wool."

An hour later, Edgar Miller dropped by to chat. "I've developed these." He showed me a collection of pointed tools made from antler bones and varying in size from very tiny to large. "We can use these for leather work and for sewing. Here's my first leather hide."

He unrolled it and let Raven feel it. "Soft and supple," Raven said.

"For pants and shirts. Made from the caribou-like animal they butchered for meat last year. I'd like to start up a leather-making business. We're going to need really warm clothing, especially during the winters."

"Excellent ideas. Have you got someone who can turn these into pants and shirts?"

"Well, not yet. First step is to provide enough hides to use. As you can see, one hide isn't enough for either pants or a shirt. Except maybe for a child. I'll ask around and see if someone would like to take these and turn them into clothing. Perhaps heavy coats. I can see them being made with a wool lining for extra warmth."

"Brilliant idea. I hadn't thought of making winter coats. This would be ideal. Leather won't soak up moisture. Have you seen anything else? Visions, perhaps?"

"Well, yes, but I didn't want to mention visions. You'd think I was bonkers. But I see it as a multi-faceted industry. We need the meat for food. I can turn the hides into leather and make bone tools. Others can take the leather and tools and turn out warm clothing and winter coats. Nothing gets wasted, except the internal guts."

"Okay, excellent planning. XO Koralsky is organizing the caribou actions. I'll tell her about your needs. Work with her to coordinate actions. So glad you thought of these ideas. Well done."

With a broad grin, he left to find Faith. Raven watched him go. *Is everyone having visions? Hallucinations? What's going on? None of the visions are the same thing. Weird. Wonder if the doctors know about this? Is it an actual phenomenon?*

"Ah, there you are," Faith said. "Been looking for you. Did Edgar see you about making leather? Okay. Good. Yes, I'm following up on something someone said before they left us last year. That the caribou seemed tame. We don't have many horses and our need for wagon transport is huge. So I'm going to try to tame some and get them used to either being ridden or pulling a wagon. That is, if you don't have other plans for me right now. I'll still be overseeing the cruiser's actions, though. Is anyone building the wagons we need?"

"I'm still working on that one. Say, did you have

dreams about using caribou like this?"

"Sort of. Kept them to myself. Don't want the others to get the idea I'm seeing things. Good luck with the wagons. We sure need them."

Raven remembered one of her security guards knew something about wagons. He'd talked about historical re-enactments. She found Dirk Vega helping Hans dismantle another section of the cruiser.

"Can I borrow Dirk for a few minutes?"

Hans chuckled. "Yeah, but only for a few. This bulkhead will make a lot of tools once we get it removed and cut up."

"So what's up?" Dirk asked. "Zita's not in trouble, is she?"

She was Dr. Wu's nurse. "No, nothing about her. I remember you once were talking about wagons. Historical wagons."

"Sure. Loved them. Took part in a re-enactment once. Why?"

"We need a lot of wagons. Are they complicated to make?"

"Mostly, it's a box. But we don't have boards for boxes. Then, there are the wheels. Ancient wheels tried to use giant wooden wheels, crude and not very effective. Spoked wheels with iron rims are the best. Long lasting, too, and don't require complex axles. Then there are the tongues. You hitch the horses to them. Tongues are difficult to make as they have to give freely in many directions, especially when turning the wagon. Last, we need harnesses. Usually complex leather works. A solid wagon is a complex affair to make. Always loved them. When I was a boy, I had six miniature toy wagons. Collected them, actually. Why?"

"We need a bunch of wagons. I need to find someone who would be interested in making us some. You're the most qualified person I've come across. Want to take on that challenge once you finish helping Hans?"

"Sure. Did you know XO Koralsky is planning to train caribou to pull wagons? Don't think we can get the

Spaniards to part with more horses."

"Yes, just talked with her about doing that. As you work out what you need to build us a wagon, let me know. I'll see you get the help you want."

"Talk about fun. I've always wanted to experiment with wagons. I've got all kinds of ideas of what they could look like bouncing around my mind. Always have had. I'll draw up some initial plans later today and see what you think about them. Gotta be able to haul coal and iron ore from the mines, right?"

"Exactly. Plus trading with the other groups. Thanks."

"Hey, speaking of trading, talk to Henry Banks. He's been dreaming of being a traveling trader, going from one group to the next. Always traveling with his wagon. I know we don't yet have horses or wagons, but he's your man when you do."

Raven found Henry working with Ace and borrowed him for a quick chat. "Dirk Vega said you dreamed of being a traveling salesman with your own wagon."

He flushed. "Well, sort of. After the other groups split off from us, I realized there's money to be made as a trader, visiting each group, round and round. I'd have my own fancy wagon and team. I would get items from the Germans to sell to the other groups, and so on. Of course, when winter came, I'd stay over with one group that I was at. I know. Bit of a pipe dream, but it'd sure be a lot of fun. I'd get to see so much of Landfall. That would be my ideal job on this world. But hells, we don't even have wagons or many horses yet. Just a dream I have."

"Great. I have folks working on building wagons and animals to pull them. Once we get some, I'll hold you to doing the trading for us. We will need to visit each group, trading for things we and others need. I think you have a brilliant idea there, Henry. With any luck, you'll be off making your rounds by fall."

"You really think we'll have wagons and horses by then? I'm looking forward to that!"

As Raven walked back, she pondered all the people

and their visions. Was this a new phenomenon? Or just people being cooped up all winter. She decided to pay a visit to Dr. Wu.

Chapter 16 A Visit with the Doctor

Raven visited Dr. Marshall Wu for her monthly checkup. “Not sure why we need to keep checking me over. I feel fine. Baby bulge is getting bigger.”

“It’s critical we’re alerted at the first sign of anything going wrong with these pregnancies. We have neither the gynecological skills nor equipment for neonatal care. We’ll be lucky to handle normal child births. If anything goes wrong...”

After a pause, he said, “We can’t afford to lose any woman of childbearing age or any babies. So humor us.”

Dr. Kelly Johnson walked in. “Ah, Miss Cooper. Here for your two-month checkup. Have a seat.”

After the usual screening tests and questions, Dr. Wu asked, “Any more of those low-grade headaches?”

“Some, but they pale compared to the growing baby sensations. Why?”

“We want to do another scan, because we think it important to monitor the pituitary gland enlargement. We’ve been doing these scans on everyone,” Dr. Johnson said. “Ever since we discovered the gland’s unexpected and sudden growth in some of our people.”

“Some? Not all?” Raven asked.

“Had any unusual feelings, emotions, strange visions, anything out of the ordinary?” Dr. Wu asked.

“Strange that you mentioned visions. Many people have been using that word of late. One guy had visions of how to make the wagons we need, and I okayed his plans. Is that what you mean?”

“Yes, something like that. We have a theory about this.”

“Please, share it. It’s really strange that so many people could suddenly come up with brilliant ideas or plans that greatly aid our survival, and in such a timely manner.”

"Since we first discovered the unexplained, enlarged glands, we've been subjecting each person to the head scans. Something is definitely going on, but not with everyone. Half our population, that is some two hundred fifty, has enlarged pituitary glands, like yours. The other half has shown no such signs—theirs are perfectly normal."

Dr. Johnson said, "Which has us baffled. Why would half our population suddenly have enlarged pituitary glands while the other half shows no such effect? Is it something you ate? Drank? Just what's causing this growth?"

"And what's the effects of the enlarged glands?" Dr. Wu asked. "What is the long-term impact of the enlarged glands? Short-term effects? Good or bad? Is this something we need to remedy? Should we attempt to find methods to reduce the gland's size? As your medical people, it's our duty and obligation to find the answers."

"But," Dr. Johnson said, "we lack nearly every tool we'd need to accurately study this phenomenon and find the answers you need. About all we can do with our ship's medical machines is to diagnose the common illnesses and injuries expected on a warship."

"We're doing the best we can. Gathering all the data we can. Who has the enlarged glands and who doesn't? What emotional effects have people been having? Overly tired? That's why all the questions when you first arrived today. We're asking everyone those same questions, trying to correlate or come up with a cause-effect relationship."

Raven said, "I expect many are having emotional troubles. Lord, we're stranded on an uninhabited planet with little chance of long-term survival, especially shocking because of how brutal the winters are on this world."

"Well, yes," Dr. Wu said, "that's quite true. We're not trained or equipped to handle mental illnesses. So we're steering clear of that area, in so much as we can. We can't do much to help someone who feels hopeless—that there's no future."

"Actually, Miss Cooper, you're the one who's been

highly successful in dealing with those problems—the mental health of us survivors. No, we're amassing statistical evidence of effects, hoping to correlate those with the gland growth. Mind you, we have absolutely no idea what is causing the pituitary glands to more than double in size. Defies all logic."

"But," Dr. Johnson said, "some effects are showing a strong correlation with pituitary gland size. As long as our computers can run, we're storing the data and running comparison graphs. Here's the correlation between anger issues versus gland sizes. As you can see, some members of both groups have anger problems. Not everyone, of course. But so far, people with enlarged glands have ten percent more anger issues.

"This one shows tiredness or unusual fatigue. About the same results. Anyone can feel fatigued. But there's a slight tendency for increased fatigue in enlarged gland people."

He showed ten more graphs of other minor physical effects, which displayed a similar correlation.

"But one aspect we hadn't thought of but kept appearing so frequently that we had to incorporate it into our study. Visions or hallucinations. We're not sure what exactly to call them."

Raven smiled. "I'd call them hallucinations. Mine was of the far distant future when I was on my deathbed. I sure wouldn't call that a vision. But so many I've met are calling theirs visions. Sorry. Go ahead."

"Here's the graph of those. As you can see, people with normal glands have almost no visions or hallucinations or unexplained phenomenon. But those with enlarged glands have a seventy-five percent chance of having them."

"Wow!"

Dr. Wu said, "Upon additional checking, they do not have these visions often and the visions are always on the same topic or subject. It's not like the visions happen all the time or that the vision topics vary."

Raven said, "I've kind of associated the visions a

person told me they had with what they most wanted to do to help our survival. Like the man who wants to build wagons."

"That ties in with our findings, too, Miss Cooper," Dr. Wu said.

"So these enlarged glands—they are a big help to our survival?"

"We really can't answer that one. How could we evaluate that intangible? We can only deal with observable facts. Dealing with visions or whatever these are is stretching our skills beyond what we're used to handling. Give us a broken bone any day. But this? Gods, we don't know what we're dealing with. Just trying to get some handle on whether it's a benefit or a disaster that we need to cure somehow."

"Is there a cure for these enlarged glands?"

Dr. Johnson frowned. "Well, no, not really. If we have to shrink them, that's beyond our knowledge, unless we could find out what's causing the pituitary glands to double."

"No ideas on that?"

"No, sorry."

"Half of us have it and the other half don't? Any theories why that is?"

"Well, yes. That's what I meant by saying we're developing a theory. Mind you, we do not have any equipment to actually study this or prove it," Dr. Johnson said. "It was Dr. Wu's bright idea. Tell her, doctor."

"Just a theory," Dr. Wu said. "The abnormal pituitary gland growth could be tied to the person's genetic makeup."

"Huh?"

"We're dealing with humans from England, Scotland, Germany, Northern Spain, and Basque, which is the most ancient and interesting genetic group. The defining genetic markers is the Haplogroup R1b, widespread in the Basque and Spanish and English groups, likely coming from the Yamnaya migration. The Germans often have the I1a marker from a different people's migration.

"It's a shame our five groups have separated. They could add enormously to our study. We'd expect the Basque and Northern Spain to have the greatest number of people whose pituitary glands are enlarged now."

"Wait. How can you come to that postulate?"

Both men sighed. Dr. Johnson said, "When this phenomenon first began and we started collecting data, we wondered why some were not affected. So we collected information about each person's ancestry, as best as they could recall. Of course, people intermarry. You, for example, cannot trace any distant relative to anywhere but England. Others from London have German and Scandinavian relatives in their family tree.

"We treated those with a Basque ancestry as most closely tied to the Yamnaya people from the steppes. They have Haplogroup R1b in their genetic material. Yes, so does most everyone else in Europe and England. But from what we can get off the computer, the Germans have a much greater I1a contribution than the rest.

"If we could do a DNA analysis, we could pin this down. Our best guess right now, and mind you, it's just a theory, is that those people who have a healthy amount of the R1b in their genes are being affected the most by that which is causing the pituitary gland's growth. Those who have a lesser amount are unaffected. Show her the tentative graph."

Dr. Wu displayed another graph showing that correlation, which seemed pretty convincing to Raven.

"None of this proves anything. It's suggestive. But," Dr. Wu said, "maybe those currently not affected will take longer for the unknown agent to affect their pituitary glands. Perhaps in a couple of years, we can pin down that aspect. It would also help if we could study the other groups' people. If our theory is correct, the Germans should have the fewest people with enlarged pituitary glands."

Dr. Johnson said, "But is this effect even important? That some of you have visions or hallucinations or imaginings—is that even significant? If we had some Russians, Polish, Ukrainians, or Scandinavians with us, that would really solidify this theory as none of those ought to be affected by whatever is causing this phenomenon."

"And we could be completely wrong," Dr. Wu said. "And the growth has nothing to do with the person's genetic makeup. We're grasping at straws."

"Well, right or wrong, you've amassed some compelling evidence that something in our genetic material could be a factor. Well done, both of you. Incredible work. Keep on collecting the data. I don't know if this enlarged gland effect is significant or vital, but it's well worth studying. I wonder if our babies will inherit larger glands from us. Or if that's even an important thing."

"Look, it could be important, Miss Cooper. The pituitary gland can control many body functions. Rather like the master gland. So a larger one could well be a survival enhancement. Time may furnish more answers. One thing is clear, Miss Cooper."

"What's that?"

"You are the single person who has kept us alive and surviving against impossible odds," Dr. Wu said. "When we landed, I became convinced this was the end. This world offered nothing for our survival. No homes, food, shelter. No infrastructure. Like so many, I secretly felt we were doomed, likely dying of starvation with little hope for a livable future. You alone stepped into that vacuum and led us on a survival path. Honestly, the future now looks survivable to me, all thanks to your efforts."

"I don't know about all that. Others have done the actual work. Even the XO stepped up to help. But thanks for telling me I'm helping. I appreciate it. Between us, I don't want to spend another winter in that cramped spaceship if we have an alternative."

Chapter 17 Trading

Midsummer, trading representatives from the other groups began arriving. Gill Macnab, from the far northwestern region representing the Scotts, arrived first. He came via a horse which pulled a crude wagon.

"I've a load of wool to trade for any fresh garden produce or grains or livestock feed or even some of the ship's blue goo emergency rations. We nearly starved to death last winter," the redhead explained to Koralsky, whom I'd placed in charge of dealing with traders.

"Thank heavens," Faith said. "We really need lots of wool. While our people unload and examine your load, how about sharing the last of our coffee? We'd like to hear how you and your people managed the past winter, and our doctors would also like to chat with you as well."

"Sure thing. God, real coffee! How are we going to survive without coffee?"

While women unloaded and examined the bales of wool and worked out what would be a fair trade, Gill eagerly talked with Faith, Raven, and Dr. Wu, who joined them.

"The caves saved us," he said. "We didn't know how many cords of firewood we needed. Almost didn't have enough. We wouldn't have had nearly enough if Carson Macintosh hadn't had visions of the amount we needed. When the heavy snows came prohibiting us from cutting more firewood, we fell short two cords from what Carson thought we should have laid in. We discovered if you go back deep enough into those caves, the ground warms up some, enough so that a fire keeps you warm. The ceilings are high enough to keep the smoke away from us. It drifts to small openings in the ceilings.

"Finlay Macnab had an idea of how many fish we'd need. Dried fish and caribou. Eaton Macdonald correctly estimated how much fodder the sheep needed."

Dr. Wu interrupted him. "Did these men have visions about how much you needed? Or imaginations?"

"Well, sort of. Some of us have had proper visions, doc. I've had visions of coming down here to trade. I might have imagined having coffee. But I didn't think there would be any left by now."

"About how many of your people have had some sort of visions or hallucinations or imaginings?"

"Oh, I recon about half of us have had some sort of dreams. Not much else to do during the winter. Of course, we'll be better prepared for this winter. And we'll have a lot of babies fairly soon, too."

"Would you let us run a CAT scan on your head? I'd really like to give you a thorough checkup," Dr. Wu said. "If so, I'll give you a lengthy letter to take back to your medical doctor."

He agreed. While the doctors checked him out, Faith worked out the trade and had the goods ready for Gill to inspect and load in his wooden wagon-like affair.

When Gill came out of the spaceship, he carried a letter to their doctor, which he stuffed in his shirt pocket. After verifying what Faith offered in trade, he loaded his wagon and headed back northwest, leading his horse.

"He's going to need new boots after walking over a thousand miles to get here. And then back again," Faith said.

Raven said, "Gosh, I forgot about footwear. I'll make an announcement at the next group meeting. Perhaps someone will have some experience with boot making."

Faith chuckled. "Raven, you always have new things to announce and find workers for. What would we do without you?"

Dr. Wu joined them. "The scan confirmed Gill's pituitary gland is enlarged, too. I sent our analysis back with him to share it with their medical doctor. I want to test anyone from the other groups who might drop by."

Raven said, "Well, if your theory about the R1a thing is correct, we'd expect the Scotts to have enlarged glands, too, along with the Basques and Spaniards. Perhaps not so much with the Germans."

"Exactly so."

After she left the doctors, a mild-mannered young man waved a paper at her. "Excuse me, Miss Cooper. We've never met. My name is Homer Norton. I've been helping Ace build the castle. I showed him this, and he sent me to find you."

"Hello, Mr. Norton. What's with the paper?"

"It's proof my vision works. It's the first piece of paper made on Landfall."

Raven took the paper from Homer. "It's rather brown and rough. But damn it! It's a paper I could write on! Okay, how'd you make it? We really need paper if I'm ever going to get schools going for kids."

"Wood chips. With all the wood chopping. I gathered up all I could. In my spare time. Didn't want it to slow down the castle building. None of us do. We don't want to spend another winter cooped up in that cruiser, or rather, what's left of it. Then I soaked the chips and pounded them into a pulpy mass using some discarded stones Ace couldn't use in the castle. When I got it pulverized enough, I let a lot of the water dry out before scooping the mass onto a flat piece of granite Ace didn't want. Then I placed a very heavy flat slab on top of it and let it dry for several days. I didn't waste any that squished out the sides. Collected that and will reuse it for the next piece of paper. This is what you get once it's fully dried. I know it's rather dark, so I will experiment more on how to make it whiter."

"Super well done, Homer. I'm going to find a replacement for you on Ace's work crew. I want you to devote yourself to paper production full-time. Because of this, our grandchildren can teach their children to write and read, to say nothing of learning many new things. Mind if I keep this paper? I want to show it to the entire group at the next meeting."

One very pleased young man shook Raven's hand heartily and left, skipping along.

"You made his day," Faith said, joining her. "What was that all about?"

Waving the brownish paper, she said, "He's invented a way to make paper. Now we have a way to pass on our knowledge to our grandchildren's children. Once the computer system goes down, there goes all our education programs. We'll need people teachers again. Which is why I'm here. Well, I was headed to New Terra to teach high school physics, but..."

Two days later, traders from the Basques and Spaniards arrived. They'd traveled here together, claiming safety in numbers. They brought two pregnant cows and horses to trade. Raven learned the Basques had made a sheltered bay their new base of operations. The ocean moderated winter's ferocity while providing bountiful fishing. The trader explained many men were building boats, as others handled the cattle. They'd survived the winter by building a dozen long houses, which housed extended families under one roof. This year, he said construction of sturdier, warmer homes had begun.

Their southern neighbors, the Spaniards, had done the same, but were now erecting stone homes. Certain areas of the southern rolling hills contained more rocks than dirt. They suspected it had been a glacial deposition area.

That predator animals roamed the rolling hills surprised Raven the most. Big cat-like animals, while rare, threatened the cattle, but the horses outran them. These, they called cougars, since that was the nearest known animal that looked like these predators. The second predator: wolves, or animals that resembled them. Both these predators had very thick hairy coats and large pads on their feet that allowed them easy travel over deep snow-covered ground. Both types made their homes in dug out burrows in hillsides.

Thus, for trade items, both wanted metal for arrowheads. "We've made excellent longbows, but it's the arrow tips we need to protect our cattle and horses."

Raven made sure that they returned with as much

aluminum scrap as they could transport. She also instructed Hans to make arrowheads for local usage, even though neither wolves nor cougars had yet been spotted around Three Peaks.

When the doctors checked the two men, again, they found some of these groups had developed visions, adding further validity to the prevailing theory.

When the two German traders arrived a week later, Raven sensed anger from the men. Yes, they brought gold and bronze ingots to trade, but not steel or iron. When Raven pressed them, they refused to say why they weren't trading the steel they'd forged, but the weaker bronze. While unspoken, she got the distinct impression the Germans made steel weapons and would give the weaker metal, bronze, to the other groups, leaving them with the stronger weapons.

They wanted blasters and disintegrators from the ship, which XO Koralsky refused to give. Again, from their reactions, Raven guessed that they knew this request would be refused. They settled for metal sections of the ship along with crop seeds, since they could get another crop producing before winter. They also wanted a laptop, even though Raven explained its battery would only last a couple of hours before needing a recharge. To handle that, they also took one small portable generator with three gallons of fuel.

The doctors gave the men free medical checkups, which pleased the angry men. This time, neither had heard of people having hallucinations or visions, further clues of the genetic effects. But they also described the two predators which lived in the lower elevations of the Lower Helades. They called them lions and wolves, which is why they claimed to have wanted weapons to protect themselves.

The men spent three days visiting and studying how the English fared. Then, they packed up and headed for their home in the northeast. They'd been gone only a few hours when Hans ran up to Koralsky.

"Boss, someone's raided the armory and stolen two

blasters and a disintegrator pistol!"

"How?" she asked.

"Come see. They must have cut through the locks. Probably during the night. No one's seen a thing."

Raven joined them at the armory, where one lock had been cut with bolt cutters, found lying in a corner.

"They didn't even take a charger," Hans said. "So that's something, at least."

"Makes no sense," Faith said. "The disintegrator pistol is only good for five shots, and the blaster can fire a dozen times before needing a recharge. Without electricity, they've got no way to recharge them."

"But they took a small generator," Raven said.

"Shit. Well, it's limited-use weapons. Unless they can manufacture fuel, the generator can only run maybe a dozen hours on the fuel we gave them. Considering recharge times are one and a half hours, that gives them maybe eight recharges. We don't trade them more fuel next time."

Raven said, "Agreed. Seems we still can't trust the Germans. I suggest we use the bronze to make pots, pans, and utensils, not to make swords."

Faith said, "I'm counting on our people to turn that iron ore into steel. We need to show the Germans they don't have a monopoly on steel weapons."

"Right. They know we still control the armory, so it's not like they're going to attack us."

"Even if they wanted to get all the remaining fuel, that, too, will eventually run out, making all these weapons useless," Faith said. "I just hope no one invents gunpowder or dynamite. What are we going to do with the gold?"

"I had thought we'd make coins out of it," Raven said. "But right now, we've no need of money. Set it aside for our children's children to use. I don't know what the Germans are going to do with all the gold they claim they've found in their area. There's nothing to buy here. We have to make everything ourselves."

A commotion brought the pair outside the ship. A man arrived with a load of coal for the winter. Cheers greeted him.

"Tons more, if'en we only had the wagons," he said. "Unload me, and I'll head back for more. Say, there are lions and wolves in the foothills of the Lower Helades."

Faith said, "Yes, we've just learned of their existence from the traders. I'm going to issue you a couple of blasters to take back with you, just in case you run into one of them."

"Thanks! When we spotted them watching our camps, we got plenty worried. Figured we'd have to fight them off with our pickaxes and shovels. They'll be thrilled to have the blasters. Just in case."

Chapter 18 Training Caribou

During the summer, Dirk Vega made progress on his wagon-making. At first, his wooden spoked wheels wore out quickly. The ability to make iron rims depended upon our ability to make iron ingots, which, though progressing, hadn't yet produced results. The new bronze ingots suggested a different route for Dirk. He confiscated some ingots.

Using hammers and granite boulders, he hammered the bronze into circular strips, measuring their diameters to be a little smaller than the wooden spoked wheels he'd made. With two made, he then lit a bonfire, laying the two rims in the blaze. Using tongs, he lifted one rim out and laid it around the rim of a wheel. That took some doing, since he couldn't touch the hot metal. Once in position, he poured water on the bronze, causing steam to rise and the bronze to shrink.

When it had cooled, he tested it. Nothing he did could pry the bronze strip from the wheel. Satisfied, he did the same to the second wheel. Then Dirk mounted the wheels onto his first two-wheeled wagon. Viola, he now had a wagon capable of transporting coal from the mines in the east to the ship.

For this, he received a round of cheers and clapping at the next group meeting. Since we're received two more horses from the Spaniards, Raven allowed another man to use two other horses to pull this new cart to the mines for more coal for the winter.

Faith Koralsky's vision had been using the caribou-like animals as horses and pack animals by taming them. Not a day passed without small groups of the animals wandering into our area, though the electric fences kept them out of the crop fields and away from their other animals. While she knew nothing about animal training or riding, her visions suggested these animals could be trained. Just not how. Then one day, she met Tina Shepherd. The two got to talking, and Faith discovered Tina had once had horses when she was growing up on a farm in Essex.

Together, the two roped one likely caribou candidate that seemed friendlier than its companions. At first, the animal reacted as a wild animal would, lunging, pulling, and trying to get away. But Tina kept talking calming words to it, while Faith found a sack of grain. The way to a caribou is through its stomach, the pair discovered. Convinced it would get more of the tasty grain, the caribou relaxed and let Tina pet it.

Thus began the taming of some caribou animals. By the time fall came, Tina had a herd of a dozen feeding out of her hand. They stuck around through the winter as long as she fed them daily.

Their anatomy required different tack from that of a horse. Clever with her hands, Tina modified a horse bridle to fit, removing the bit, turning it into a hackamore type bridle. The caribou's back was much thinner than a horse, so normal saddles wouldn't fit, so she began by riding bareback. She discovered that unlike horses, the mild-mannered caribou didn't buck and try to throw its rider off, especially when she kept feeding it tasty grains.

Faith said, "You, Tina Shepherd, are a caribou whisperer."

Both laughed.

"I seem to have a knack with them. They are more surefooted in the deep snow. We've already seen that last winter. They don't rile easily, but I expect they will when they hear a wolf or cougar coming. Next step is to see if I can convince one to pull a wagon. They're not as strong as a horse, so it'll likely take a team of two where one horse would suffice. Have to see."

Things became unavoidably delayed late summer. Both Raven and Faith's babies were due to arrive. Besides, both found it hard to get around those last days.

"I'm a veritable blimp!" Raven said, struggling to get up out of the shared bed.

"Same here. Maybe it wasn't such a bright idea to get both of us pregnant at the same time. Shit. I can't get up! Little help."

"I think we've a water leak in here," Raven said, as she helped pull Faith into a sitting position.

"It's all down—shit, your water just burst. Baby time, Raven."

"Oh! Now that's a cramp. I think it's coming and I'm a mess. Help me clean up and change before we head to the medical bay."

When the pair showed up, Dr. Wu said, "Ah, guess it's time for the babies."

"Just me right now. Got cramps. Water broke. Hope everything's okay," Raven said. "Is this going to hurt a lot?"

"If you can just relax and let your body do its thing, then perhaps not. Nurse, stand by with..."

"Already on it," she said.

"I've heard it's painful," Faith said.

"For some, it is. But I always try to be optimistic, especially since from now on, we have limited resources. Stay as calm and relaxed as you can. You body must have time to expand enough to allow the baby to come out. That's our objective. Breathing helps some women."

As the minutes flowed on, Raven asked more questions, her analytical mind struggling to digest all these new sensory inputs. She tried to focus her mind on something else. "I'm going to start teaching physics this winter."

"Hey, that's good to hear. We need to get educations going. Soon the ship's computers will cease. All that knowledge will be lost. I wish there was a way Dr. Johnson and I could relay all that we know to the next generation of doctors, but we've yet to figure out a way without the computers."

Ignoring a new cramp, she said in an attempt to keep her mind off this, "Can you print off some key tech details new trainees could use when the computers are dead?"

"We thought of that, Miss Cooper, but there's a severe computer paper shortage now. I fear we will lose so many pieces of our knowledge when the ship finally dies. So much will be lost, so much."

"I'm acutely aware of that. I've been working on ways around that. Got a guy making paper we can write on, albeit crudely. I have some making clay tablets containing elementary teaching materials like the A-B-Cs and the basic math tables for beginning students. I hope to start teaching calculus and physics to our teens during the winter. If we can find some young person who wants to become a doctor, can you take him or her under your wing and teach them enough to handle situations we're likely to have? I know it'll be dicey without your diagnostic machines. Keep in mind what they're likely to have as resources once the ship is no longer operational."

"Yes, Dr. Johnson and I came to that conclusion as well. We don't have any candidates."

"Well, I'll ask at the next group meeting. Oh, that was a big—"

"Had you distracted long enough. You have a daughter. You can hold her as soon as we clean her up."

"Oh, I'm a mother! Can I see her? Is she all there? I mean fingers, toes."

A baby cry proved she had healthy lungs.

"Yes, she's perfect. What'll you be calling her?"

"Rose. Rose Cooper."

"Well, Rose Cooper, here's your mother."

He laid the wrapped baby on Raven's stomach, but she pealed back the blanket, examining Rose's body for herself.

"Thanks, Dr. Wu. I got so distracted I didn't pay attention to my body's cramps. Clever of you."

He chuckled. "I only hope the other women have as easy a child birth as you've had. My nurse will send baby clothes and cloth diapers home with you. Those are things still readily available in out cabinets. When Rose outgrows them, pass them on to the next new mother. At least until we can get clothes manufacturing going."

That night, as Rose nursed, Faith asked, "So how did it go? We didn't hear you scream or anything."

"I found the cramps most annoying, but Dr. Wu kept me totally distracted and focused on how our doctors can train a new doctor. Rose was out before I noticed it. Sneaky, but it worked with me."

Two days later, Faith went into labor. After a deal of pain, she gave birth to her son, Artur, named after her father. Once back in their shared cabin, she said, "Gods, that was no fun. And to think we have to endure this three more times."

A week later, with Rose in a baby sack, Raven checked on Tina's progress with the caribou-like animals.

"Hi, and congratulations. She's beautiful."

"Thanks. Looks like you've got this one tamed. No problems, I trust?"

"No, I'm trying to get her used to pulling wagons. Empty wagons. Then I'll move up to heavier loads. Once I'm satisfied pulling heavy loads will not harm her, then I'll hand her over to the drovers, who'll bring back more loads of coal for the winter."

After giving her more encouragement, Raven walked over to inspect how Ace's castle progressed. He'd stopped working on the second floor, focusing instead on making the ground floor large enough to handle five hundred plus people and the growing number of animals.

"So you're bringing my daughter out to see her daddy working?"

"Well, that, but more to see if you think we'll be staying in the castle this winter or not."

He sighed. "Nope, not this winter, but next winter for sure. I had to make it five times the size I initially planned for. As long as I can keep the disintegrators charged up so I can cut the granite, we'll stay on target. That section there where we can house the animals—that section will be ready for them. No more smelly critters inside the ship. Had enough of that last winter. They'll be safe in there, plus I'm allowing for the storage of fodder in there as well. Good thing we don't have five hundred horses or five hundred cows. Chickens I can handle. Lots less space."

"Okay, I'll let everyone know we winter over in the ship again. Will check with Hans to make sure there's enough power to keep us warm this winter. You know, in my vision, your castle ends up with five stories, with towers and everything."

Ace laughed. "I'm a dreamer, now that I can't fly. No chance of building a new spaceship. Not in my lifetime or even my kids'. Well, you sure are making one fantastic difference, even if we won't be moving in until next summer."

Chapter 19 Second Winter and School

Ace had the castle ready to store the animals for the winter months, along with three families who volunteered to be their caretakers. One section held all the coal we'd mined this year, so we knew they and the animals would be warm. We also tied a wire line from the castle to the ship, just in case someone needed to make that journey. Because of the snow depth and whiteout conditions, people could get lost.

This left much more space in what remained of the cargo holds to store this year's crops and seed for the spring planting. Everyone complimented Raven for her foresight in utilizing the castle, freeing up ship space. The harvest bounty exceeded anyone's prediction. If only we had a way to send some to the other groups. We could only hope they'd be in good shape this winter.

The year marked the thirtieth new addition to our population. A new tradition had sprung up this past fall when more women had their babies. A hearty round of applause from the group acknowledged the births, as this punctuated our intense desire to make our survival on solid footings. And as we closed the bay doors for the winter, Raven accepted thirty women's requests to have a baby in the coming year, though she insisted they have a full checkup with the doctors before giving the okay.

Once things settled down, Raven opened the first school. Passing on our knowledge to our children roused everyone's concerns, for each had skills or specialized knowledge that without our educational computers would become lost in one generation. How could you study or know about genes if you had no medical machines and needed equipment, such as microscopes? Our medical doctors, engineers, and astronomers felt this loss of knowledge acutely.

Until now, our children could study using the ship's

computer education libraries, but like most kids, being outside and doing useful tasks or just playing games took priority. And if truth be said, we needed all the help we could get these past two years. But now Raven insisted the children dive back into their studies, if only during the winter months. In all honesty, there was little else for kids to do on that cramped cruiser.

With space at a premium, especially since over half the ship had been dismantled by this time, Raven decided to have an early grades class (1-7) in the morning and a later grades class (8-12) in the afternoon. She and Faith handled these older teens, while she found four volunteers to teach the younger kids who required much closer supervision and instruction.

Faith Koralsky taught history, civics, the Federation of Planets' doctrine, sociology, and math up to calculus. Raven taught calculus and higher math, along with various sciences. They divided the class in half. Each took half the class for half day, afternoon sessions. This way, the pair could reach all the kids. The bridge became the classroom, though they blocked off the communications center and life support consoles.

The morning sessions were held in here as well, though they grouped the kids into four distinct groups, based on what they currently knew.

Raven looked at her first group of teens, took a deep breath, glanced at the sleeping Rose, and began.

"Welcome to your first calculus class. I'm Raven Cooper, but you probably already know that." Chuckles and smiles came her way.

"I also know many of you believe this to be an impossibly hard math subject, but many of you also know it's vital to any real understanding of engineering and physics, in particular. I know I had an awful time with my first lengthy calculus course. In fact, it only made some sense when I took Advanced Calculus, when I realized my first textbook made the subject impossible to understand. I hope to remedy that from the beginning.

"Let's start with the two key symbols that pervade

all of calculus. The first comes in many forms, such as *dx*, *dy*, or *dt*. It means a tiny, little bit of whatever the letter stands for. Take *dx*. *X* often refers to the horizontal axis coordinate. So *dx* means a tiny, little bit of a change along the x-axis. And with *dt*, *t* often represents time, so *dt* means a tiny, little bit of a change in time. When you see this, *dx/dt*, it means a tiny bit of a change in position during a tiny bit of time. Yes, it's that simple. Sometimes you will see *df*, where *f* represents a function, and you're asking for a tiny bit of a change in the function.

"Then there is this symbol: ∫. It means the sum of all the little bits. Sometimes the range to sum is given as from point a to point b or from 0 to infinity. Why is this important? If I drop this marble down this ramp, how long will it take to hit those marbles at ramp's end, given this launching point is 1.25 meters above the base with the group of marbles? Ah, some of you have said it's just gravity accelerating the marble. And some of you know what gravity's amount is on the surface of Earth, right?"

Someone yelled, "Duh, 9.8 meters per second per second. Everyone knows that."

"I agree with you. But we're not on Earth, unfortunately, and in so darn many ways. So what's gravity here? If you are flying a spaceship, what's the effect of gravity when you are one mile above the Earth?

"The answers to these questions and a million more can be worked out using calculus, by observing and measuring how much of a little bit of a change happens in a little bit of time.

"This also impacts simple engineering, all the way to complex engineering situations. Let's take the very first one that we faced after the ship landed on Landfall, when animals filled our cargo holds. What did they do?"

"They put up electric fences to keep them penned up," a lad said.

"Exactly. But did they have an infinite supply of these electric fences? No. They only had a specific amount. I know because I helped them set up the fences. Let's say you have 420 feet of fence to install to hold your animals and you want to enclose the largest area, so the animals have room to move around, and it should be a rectangle with four sides. What dimensions do you lay out?

"First, we need the formula for the area of a rectangle, which from geometry we know is length times width or if we use our usual coordinate system, its *area* = *X Y*. Here our *f* is the area function and we want to pick *x* and *y* such that we get the largest area. That is, the maximum of the function which is the area formula. But we also have a limited amount of fence, so we also have $420 = 2X + 2Y$ to handle. We can simplify the problem by solving for either *X* or *Y*. In this case, $Y = (420 - 2X)/2$ or just $210 - X$. And using that in the area formula, we get the $Area = 210X - X^2$.

"What we want to solve this problem is how much a tiny bit of the area changes per a tiny bit of *X*. That's what taking a derivative of a function means. We'll start learning how to do this first. In this case $dA = 210 - 2X$. We will also see to get the maximum or minimum points of a function involves setting this equation to 0. So that we find $0 = 210 - 2X$ or $X = 105$. That also means *Y* is also 105 and we have a square whose area is 105 x 105 square feet.

"This is what I calculated for the farmers when they set up their fences, giving their animals the maximum space to move around in. So many real-world problems can be solved with calculus. That's what we're going to learn about. Then, you can use these skills to develop a myriad of answers in physics, astronomy, and engineering. So let's get started on learning how to do derivatives."

When the class period ended, Tina came up and said, "Gosh, Miss Cooper, that makes so much more sense than my official math text. I'd given up ever learning calculus. I guess I'm not stupid after all."

"No, you certainly are not. I fought it all the way through my first year calculus course, claiming none of it made any sense. Then I learned they were using a really poor textbook. That, combined with a professor that I couldn't understand, spelled disaster for me. See you tomorrow afternoon."

The bitter cold taxed the life support system, that and the volume of snow, which soon became waist deep just outside the ship. Hans monitored the weather and the power supply daily, working out how long the power would last without new nuclear fuel rods. Like Raven and Faith, he worried it might not make it through the winter. If it died during the winter, then what?

During the mornings, while others taught the younger children, Raven met with various adults, planning for the spring activities. Who should do what and when required coordination and organization. Getting in the crops early, acquiring tons of coal, and finishing enough of the castle's ground floor took top priority, since she suspected the power supply wouldn't last a third winter. They didn't have enough ion engine fuel to power portable generators through a winter, and she wanted to keep the shuttle and power tools working as long as possible before everything had to be done by hand.

Raven and many others dreaded the day when the ship's sources of power and recharging ended. Everyone would feel the heavy significance of that day. Yet, Raven knew that day grew closer, and she redoubled her efforts to get as much done in advance as possible, suspecting that momentous day would come before the next winter.

That also weighed heavily on Ace, who oversaw the castle construction and its enormous amount of work. His grand design of five stories, complete with towers, had been altered to a single story able to house their growing collection of animals and a thousand people. Well, at least six hundred before the next winter came. Each suite and area came with its own chimney in which coal would provide warmth and cooking facilities. Then, he realized he'd forgotten about lighting and begged Raven and Faith for help. Until now, he'd run wires from the ship, powering up many work lights.

"Guys, I totally forgot about lighting. Those suites are going to be quite dark. Not much light comes in the mica sheet windows. Little help here."

The solution to that didn't happen until the spring

traders began making their rounds. The Basques found an oil source from a giant fish they caught in their bay. It burned slowly and gave off a yellowish light. Raven jumped on that, striking a deal to have them bring a large quantity on their next trade. The Germans also brought their latest discovery to trade: a low-grade oil seeping up from a field near the Lower Helades. Again, Raven made a deal to get a large quantity delivered before winter came. With that established, she had others turn the copper ore into oil lanterns.

Chapter 20 Hanna Stroebel

With her sarcasm and constant pessimism, Hanna Stroebel grated on everyone's nerves that first summer. However, when her Uncle Ingel led the Germans off to claim Minen as their new land, her brother, Bart, went with them. But Hanna refused to leave the ship, so her uncle abandoned her, claiming no one wanted her and her rotten attitude.

After they left the sixteen-year-old, another young teen befriended her: Ralph Riggs. Unskilled, Ralph worked in the galley, doing dishes after every meal and helping the ship's chef when needed. He enticed Hanna to join him.

"Surely, you don't want these hands to wash dishes, do you?"

"No, I'll do the messy part, Hanna. When the dishes come out of the washer, you stack them where they belong. This way, we're doing our part to help."

"Well, okay, blondie," she said with a wry grin. True, Ralph had longish blonde hair, but she soon found him amiable company. The adults often ignored her, which she preferred. But she found a kindred spirit in Ralph, who never judged her, even when she made angry retorts.

One day during idle hours, he asked, "So how come you didn't go north with all the other Germans? Don't like your uncle?"

She stared at him long before she sighed and answered. "Look, I really like you. So if you promise never to tell anyone else, I'll tell you."

"I promise. Pinky swear." The two crossed pinky fingers.

"This," she said, sweeping her arms around encompassing the ship and all, "is *beyond* the pits. There's not a damned thing here. But—but if there is even the tiniest, remotest chance a ship will find us and rescue us, I aim to be right here and not miss that chance. My damned dad got me into this mess and blew his brains out. That's the only time in my life I cheered my dad. No, if any rescue ever comes, it'll be focused on this cruiser. So I'm *never*, ever going to leave the vicinity of the ship. I aim to be rescued and taken back to real civilization. That's why."

"That makes perfect sense, Hanna. I'm glad Miss Cooper is having us stay with the ship, too. You're not as dumb as you make others believe. And pretty too."

She huffed before smiling. "Well, I so wanted to be like my mom. Gosh, she was really beautiful. I was five when she died. Fell down some stairs. I used to snuggle up with her. She told me marvelous stories. Felt totally safe when around her. I even helped brush out her long black hair before bed. I miss her so much, Ralph, so very much."

"I'm so sorry. No one should have their mother die when they're still kids. I know I'd miss mine. If she died, that is. So she was pretty like you?"

"Well, one day I will be as pretty as she was, Ralph. I know I will. I so want to be just like her. I remember one Christmas party. When she walked into the room wearing her billowing blue gown, she lit up everyone's face. I watched how awed everyone was, men and women. They all were in awe of my mother."

"Wish I'd have known her. She sounds like a wonderful person to be around."

"Thanks. She told me that one day I could become as beautiful as she, but that I had to wait until I was eighteen and of age. Something about Dad wouldn't approve. I never understood what she meant. Ralph, I so miss her, even today. She had the most gorgeous gowns and tall heels. I've never seen anyone who looked even close to her beauty. I swear one day, Ralph, I will be just as beautiful as she was."

"But Hanna, you're beautiful now. I think you're the best-looking girl here. Among all two thousand of us."

"Well, thanks, Ralph. But I'm not even close to mother's incredible looks. No, you just wait until I can be like Mom. Then, you'll see incredible beauty. Trust me. You're quite handsome yourself, Mr. Riggs."

"Not really, Hanna. I appreciate you're telling me so, but I've never been good at sports. Or anything, actually."

"You're my best friend, Ralph. No one else here is. They all hate me. But they won't, once I become as beautiful as my mom was. Then they'll see. One day, they will, Ralph. One day."

Neither developed any special visions, though Ralph spent long hours helping with the harvesting. Then, during the long winter cooped up on the ship, the two spent most of the day in the galley, helping with chores there. Ignoring adults' orders, he made sure Hanna didn't have to do those that she didn't want to do.

The second winter, Hanna pulled Ralph aside. "You know what today is?" He shook his head. "It's my birthday. Well, as close as I can reckon it—what with being stranded on this godforsaken world. I'm eighteen! Now I can open my mother's last present for me. Come on. There's no one I'd rather share it with."

In her private cabin on the ship, she pulled out a small present wrapped in gold. A note worn from handling still taped to the outside.

"It's from Mom. The last thing I ever got from her. It's in German, so you can't read it. But it says this is to be opened on my eighteenth birthday. 'My gift to help my beautiful Hanna achieve her fondest wishes to be as beautiful as I am.' I've waited *thirteen* years to open this! Always wondering what's inside. What did she leave me?"

"Didn't your father know?"

"No, he said it was likely a dress or something. He didn't care, even less so after Mom died."

"I don't know how you could be so patient and wait for thirteen years to open it."

She giggled. "At first, I wanted to *rip* it open, but then she died. I so want to honor her memory. So even though I've been dying to open it a zillion times, I've held off. Somehow, I want you to be with me when I open the last thing I have of Mom's. You've become the most important person in my life now, and I want to share this super special moment with you."

"You're the love of my life, too. Well, it can't be a food thing in there. She'd have known food would spoil after thirteen years. It's not very heavy, but something wiggles a little inside. Maybe some heirloom jewelry or something like that."

"Dad dumped all her stuff after she died. Said it reminded him of her. He didn't give a rat's ass about my feelings. I would've loved to have had some of her things. Ah, well. I guess it's time."

She took a deep breath, held it, and began peeling back the gold wrapping paper. A birthday card rested on top of a small canister, which lay on top of a red satin gown, along with matching pumps. Choked with emotion, she read the card aloud for Ralph.

Dearest Hanna,

I know how much you want to be just like me, as beautiful as the rarest flower, a special Great Lady. But in truth, your father did this to me, making me almost helpless. At first, I hated him for doing this to me. No longer could I hug or hold you. But as time went on, I grew to appreciate how stunningly beautiful I looked. Yet, I am still nearly helpless and that's no way to live. While I know you want to be beautiful like me, you already are quite beautiful. I hope your father hasn't turned you into a helpless woman as he did me. In the canister you'll find things of yours that I dearly treasured, things that I could never touch. I looked at them for hours. So when you look at these, remember always I loved you with all my heart. You are as beautiful as you believe you are. It's not something that comes in a bottle or mutation. Remember that, and think kindly of your nearly helpless mother, my darling Hanna. I so love you.

Love,

Mom

Ralph let her take a moment to wipe her watering eyes. When she recovered, he asked, "What's in the canister? What's a special Great Lady? She must have been incredibly beautiful, just as you are, Hanna."

"I remember asking Dad that once. I think I was

about four. He said that's what Mom is. That's all I know. If we were back on Earth, we could search and find out. I guess we could see if the ship's computer knows. But I have always, always wanted to be like my mom. So whatever it is, this will let me be like she was, stunningly beautiful. That's all that matters to me."

She opened the can. Inside, she found baby shoes, a child's fancy dress, a stuffed rabbit, and a thumb drive with pictures of her as she grew from a baby.

"That's Mr. Rabbit, my favorite stuffed animal I had. I thought I'd lost him ages ago. And that's the dress I wore to my dance recital when I was five. And that's the adult red dress and heels Mom wore on that same day. She was so proud of me. Hand me my laptop. I want to see what's on this drive."

Soon, she scrolled through hundreds of pictures her personal assistant had taken of her and her mother over the years.

"Is that her? Your mom?"

Hanna nodded, fighting from tearing up.

"Gosh, you are as pretty as she is and the prettiest girl on Landfall. But now I get it. She doesn't have any arms. So she could never hold you. That's awful."

Together, they looked at all the images, Hanna describing the what and when.

That night as Ralph rose to leave, Hanna kissed him and pushed him out the door. Standing by the door, he heard her crying softly to herself.

The next morning, he visited Dr. Wu and asked him about what a special Great Lady was. The doctor looked through his files and paled when he found it.

"Son, it's an alien genetic mutation agent from Kali-D in which the victims lose their arms and grow enormous breasts. It's considered a stunning beauty enhancement for the ultra-wealthy. Sure glad we didn't bring any genetic mutation agents with us."

Raven also dropped the next day. "Happy birthday, Hanna. Heard you had a present from your mother."

"I waited so long to see what it was. Mr. Rabbit and

all my baby things. Most importantly, all these images she had of me. I know now she was helpless, so probably her personal assistant took them."

Since Hanna's eyes chose this moment to drain, she dashed off to her bathroom.

Raven said, "Ralph, I know you and Hanna have been very good for each other. You've gotten her noticeably calmed down and working with us instead against us, as she did before the Germans left for Minen. She's going to need an enormous amount of patience and understanding."

"I will look after her, Miss Cooper. Honest, I will. I love her. I can take care of her, I promise."

"I'm sure you will. Just be patient with her. She's alone now. Both parents gone. Like so many of us, a bit terrified on this world."

"Her whole life's goal has been to be like her mother. At least her memories of her mother when she was five. She never mentioned her mother didn't have any arms and hands. So confusing."

That night, Hanna invited Ralph to move into her cabin with her. Soon, both fell asleep.

Them the darkness yielded. Hanna saw her body lying in a medical machine of come kind. She watched as her arms withered and fell off as dried husks. Her ample breasts continue to swell up. Her hair turned darker, thicker, and much longer. And then Dr. Wu removed her from the machine. Ralph had laid out the clothes her mother had left for her, ready to help her dress. Dr. Wu rolled in a tall mirror, guessing she might want to see how she looked. Hanna moaned. Her eyes fluttered. Then her eyes popped wide open, realizing she'd become like her mother, the wish she'd for as long as she could remember.

She couldn't get up, but Ralph helped her sit up. Seeing her empty shoulders and massive bosom, she screamed, and Ralph quickly put his arms around her.

"This must be how beautiful your mother looked," Ralph said. "You were expecting to look like this, right?"

"Huh? I'm *helpless* like this."

“Wake up, Hanna. You’re having a bad dream.” Ralph shook her shoulders.

“Oh, I’m not helpless! Gods, what a dream! I got turned into what my mom was. Now I vaguely remember. Mom had these huge breasts. Seemed that way to me when I was five. Didn’t realize they were this gigantic. No arms. So that’s why Mom always had Janine helping her.

“She was Mom’s assistant. I remember now. I’d forgotten all about Janine. All these years, I so wanted to be like my mother.”

“But you are beautiful now. I’ll always look after you. You know that. Just a bad dream, that’s all.”

Chapter 21 Hanna's Recovery

At the end of the next day, Ralph walked her to her cabin door. As she stood facing it, her body began shaking.

"I'm terrified. Please, don't leave me. I've never felt this alone before."

"Don't worry about that. I won't leave you. I love you."

"I love you, too, but I feel so scared. Not sure of what exactly. I miss my mom but not my dad."

They sat on her small couch.

"I'd forgotten all about Mom not having any arms. Didn't seem important because Janine did everything for her."

"You dreamed of being like her for thirteen years. You look much like your mother in those pictures. I wish I could have met her. You have inherited her beauty. Anyone can see that."

"I'm suddenly recalling more images of Mom that I'd totally forgotten. It's like when I look into the mirror, I'm seeing Mom. Isn't that strange?"

"No, you are her daughter. In those images, your mother looked stunning and unforgettable. Wish I'd met her."

"You think so?" She moved her head this way and that. "Yes, Ralph, maybe I look stunning."

"You sure do. I promised Miss Cooper I'd look after you and I will."

He hugged her, and she kissed him.

"Come to bed with me, please," she said, as she disrobed and crawled into the narrow bed, beckoning him to join her.

"Oh, gods, Ralph. Running your hands across my breasts feels incredible. More. More. Oh!" She noticed he'd become quite hard, and she grinned. "Let's do it. Right now. Poke it in me. It's like I'm craving it. Please. I love you. Gods, yes. Yes." She continued to passionately kiss him as they reached climaxes.

"Indescribably good. I need that every day. Please."

Later, they showered together. "The hot water's off. We've used up our allowance. Best get out now. I'll dry us off."

Later, dried and redressed, the two sat on her bed edge again.

"Ralph, that was so wonderful. But what's going to happen to me, to us, on this desolate world? I can't depend on you for everything. That's not fair."

Ralph chuckled. "What a change in you. When we first met, you'd never even think such a thought. And now your entire attitude has changed. For the better, I think."

"Really? Yeah, you're right. Something is really changed in me. I feel so different, Ralph. How strange is that? It's like I'm a different person, though I'm not. Am I?"

"Well, you were supposed to open your present from your mom when you turned eighteen."

"Yes, I was supposed to do that. Supposed to fight against Dad. Oh, shit! Ralph, I blamed Dad for Mom's death. He knew she had a hard time with stairs and insisted she sleep in the upstairs bedroom. Meaning she had to go up and down the stairs many times a day. He could have moved her bedroom downstairs into the guest room. Looking back on it, I sensed he wanted her to fall and break her neck. Wait, more memories are coming back.

"Bart's just been born, and Dad's now demanding she become a special Great Lady. I overheard them arguing. He said, 'You've had two. So now it's time.' Mom sure didn't want to do it. Dad forced her to. No wonder I always *rebelled* against anything Dad was for. I was a bitch to him, but I didn't know why.

"Gods, Ralph! More images are coming. I couldn't have been over three at the time. He's taking Mom away to the Med Center in Aachen. I wanted her back with me and Bart. She came back, and I hugged her, but she couldn't hold or hug me anymore. I remember that first day, she had tears running down her face as I clung to her when she came home. I couldn't figure out why she couldn't hold me back. She's saying something to me. I think she said, 'Dad wants me to be stunningly beautiful for him.' Something like that. When I was four, I sat on her lap. She looked so beautiful and I told her so.

"She said, 'Yes, everyone notices me now. I'm stunningly beautiful, just as your father wishes.' And I remember saying I wanted to be stunningly beautiful when I grow up. Wait, I think I must have told her that a thousand times. Maybe that's why she gave me this present.

"Hold on a second. I'm looking at her when she first came back and then when I was five and she gave me this present. She's changed. At first, she hated what had happened to her. Two years later, she seems to embrace what had happened. I wonder what changed? I recall Dad taking her out to fancy affairs nearly every weekend. When I wanted to snuggle up to Mom, I couldn't. Pissed me off."

Ralph said, "I bet your dad didn't like that."

She chuckled. "You called that one. He even spanked me once over that. I bet since he treated her like a queen those two years, she changed her opinion of herself. Janine was always there with her, helping her with everything. I bet that's what happened. But Mom didn't want me to be like her. I bet that's why she gave me this gift."

"Boy, does that ever make sense, Hanna! I think you've uncovered the whole thing. What an awful thing for a young kid to go through. Was Bart affected by it?"

"No, Bart was oblivious to it all. I feel like a ton has lifted off of me. Like some heavy black mass is gone. Wow! I think I've blown stuff away that I didn't know was there. No wonder I feel so different. Crap! I'm still me, Ralph. I think I somehow dodged a bullet."

"How so?"

"For years, I kept going on about being like Mom. Telling Dad that every day for years. It's a miracle he didn't have me mutated too."

"Great job on spotting all those nasty memories. But you really are very beautiful. I love you. We'll figure this out."

"Hold me. I'm about to bawl my head off."

Ralph pulled her close to him, and her tears flowed for a half hour.

When she stopped, she said, "That's funny. I just remembered I never cried when Mom died. I felt sad, yes, but I didn't cry. You know, I think she found relief from her life. It can't be an enjoyable life when you're totally helpless like she was. My dad was a monster, wasn't he?"

That night, he asked, "Want me to sleep with you again?"

"Thanks. I feel so alone on this world."

When he slipped into the bed, she said, "Please, run your hands over my shoulders and body like you did last night."

As he did so, but she began kissing him. Neither could hold back on their passions. Both finished, he lay back, pulling her onto his shoulder.

"I love you," she said. "I can't believe how wonderful having you in me feels. I don't ever want it to stop." She kissed him again before both fell into a relaxing sleep.

Over breakfast the next morning, he said, "We should see about helping the others. Earn our keep, so to speak."

After eating, Ralph headed to the dishwasher machine, and Hanna followed.

"Am I supposed to put the dried dishes away?"

"Yes, I wash. You dry. Teamwork."

When she finished, a smile lit her face. "I actually *did* it. A real job. My first ever."

"Ralph, you're the greatest."

"And you are stunningly beautiful and smart. The best woman here."

Both laughed.

That night, as their lovemaking began, Ralph

suddenly could feel what Hanna felt as she experienced it. What she thought, what she wanted, what desires of the moment she craved, he saw and responded by satisfying them. Many involved using his hands to caress or touch a part of her body. But nothing prepared him to co-experience her orgasm when she came. Later, he called this their "let me in" times, which happened often. Only much later on did they both realize what Hanna had done.

As they lay together, she on his shoulders, she said, "So incredible!"

They were still in a close rapport, and Ralph glimpsed another of her childhood images that she'd just accidentally triggered.

"I just remembered something. Vaguely. When I was three. Mom had just come home as the stunningly beautiful woman. I'd wandered into her room to get a reassuring hug. Fearing monsters under my bed. She must have been crying quietly. Saw wet streaks on her face. I threw my arms around her legs, expecting her to hug me as she had always done before. She said, 'Sweetheart, from now on, you'll have to do the hugging for us both.' I think I said something like 'No, you hug me.' She said, 'I can't anymore. Daddy wants me to be a stunningly beautiful woman now. Be brave. Go back to bed.' I felt alienated from Mom, but then I blamed Dad for making her this way. I was only three. No wonder I always despised my dad."

"I'm so sorry you had to endure all that. Explains so much. I love you, and we're a team now. Just let me in all the time."

A week later, Raven stopped to chat with them. She said, "I've been watching you, Hanna. I'm amazed at how well you are adapting to life on Landfall. Keep up the good work. Oh, and Dr. Wu wants to give you another checkup. He's worried about how he can do these once we lose power and all his medical machines don't work."

The doctor did a scan to see how her pituitary gland fared. It had enlarged, just as had so many others. Yet, she didn't volunteer that she'd had any visions or hallucinations or imaginings. Unusual.

He discussed this result with Raven. She said, "Maybe the effects are private to her. Bottom line, she sure has had a wonderful personality change. She finally fits in with the rest of us."

Later, when the time came to harvest some crops, Ralph and Hanna joined in picking the beans and peas. There she was, sitting on the ground and picking off pods. While drastically slower than the other workers, she insisted on helping as she could. Again, Raven noticed this and complimented her.

"Hanna, you never cease to amaze me. Never in a million years would I have predicted you'd be out here on your butt helping pick the peas. Very well done."

"Thanks. I must do what I can to help us survive. Now I want to live. I simply won't let stupid actions ruin the rest of my life. You've let me join your group, and I will do what I can to help everyone. I once thought you'd kick me out. I sure was a bitch."

"You've earned your place here. Keep on trying. Between us, you are inspiring others with your determination to help as you can."

Weeks later, two men from Minen came to trade goods while Hanna and Ralph picked beans in the garden plot. Hanna knew the men, close associates of her uncle, but they didn't recognize her because her appearance had changed so much.

Hanna stopped picking and paled. "I gotta go warn Raven. They're here to steal blasters."

She dashed off to find Raven. Ten minutes later and out of breath from running about, she found her.

"Those men of Ingel Stroebel are here to steal blasters!"

"How do you know?"

"That's what they were thinking when they rode up and spotted the ship. You can't let them get the blasters. Please."

Raven acted, rounding up Sam and Jessica Smeltzer, the Hawker's original security team. Minutes later, the three caught the two red-handed trying to break into the armory. That was when Raven suspected Hanna might have some telepathic ability. However, she didn't press the issue out of fear of repercussions. No one liked someone prying on their private thoughts.

Chapter 22 The Castle

"Ta da! I present to you Cooper Castle!" Ace yelled, unveiling his castle to the entire group assembled to get their first tour. "Six entrances, including this one for horses and wagons. On your right are the stables and fodder storage. On your left is the banquet hall and adjoining kitchen. We're still going to have communal meals like we've been doing in the ship's galley. The rest of the first floor holds fifty suites, some designed to house four, some to house a dozen.

"Each suite has a fireplace for burning coal. Our bronze lamp maker has made a lantern for each suite. At the end of each hallway is a water well. At the other end of each hallway is a place to dump your chamber pots. They drain into an underground cistern affair. Finally, connected to the kitchen are the many small rooms holding our food supplies and either a coal pile or logs."

After a loud round of applause and cheering which Ace ate up, XO Faith Koralsky said, "We are dismantling the ship's galley. Each suite will get a share of carpeting from the ship and a portion of the extra pots, pans, dishes, and silverware—all of which have been in storage all this time. The goal is to get everyone settled into their own suite before the first ice storm. With luck, the ship will be unused this winter, left as a backup in case something goes wrong. There isn't enough power left to keep it fully heated this winter. We believe there is enough power to keep the ship just above freezing. Raven."

Raven stood and continued the prepared words. "I want to thank Ace Trundel for his tireless efforts and visions to create this solid orange castle where there was nothing before. Those of you who know Ace also know this is a work in progress. His plans call for five stories with towers and many support structures. Next season, he'll begin work on the walls for our second floor. Historical documents say it took decades to build these kinds of castles.

"We number over seven hundred of us now, but only fifty suites. If the suites were all the same size, that means we'd put fourteen people in each one. But they aren't all that large. So Faith and I have been working out where to put everyone. Wintering over in the spaceship won't work. The power won't last all winter. The plan is to put extended families together in the larger suites. Certainly, everyone will have a bed to sleep in. The big question is who to put in which suite.

"I've thought about this for weeks. I think who stays where should be your decision, not mine. Much doubling up must be done. But the first step is to actually see what these suites look like, their layout. After this tour, go back to your quarters and work out your groups. When you have, bring your list to me. Mind you, if your choices require more suites than we have, I'll have to override your choices. Everyone must have housing before winter comes. Okay, Ace, walk us through these three types of suites."

Ace said, "I have numbered each hallway, and each suite also has it's unique number. We're going down Hallway One. First up is Suite 1-1-1. The first 1 is the floor number. The second 1 is the hallway number, and the third 1 is the room number. This one is one of the largest suites. We think you can fit at least twenty people in here, maybe more."

When they reached the last suite at the end of the hallway where the water well stood, he said, "This was supposed to be a storage room for brooms, bedding, and cleaning supplies. But of necessity, it's being used to house two people. It's barely larger than a tiny ship's cabin. I know. Who's going to want to stay in a closet? But we have to get everyone inside before the ice storms begin."

"Is the only exit way back down the hallway?" someone asked.

"Aye, I'm afraid the closet people will have to do a lot of walking. I will get going on the second floor this spring, after saving the metal roof made from the skin of the cruiser. When I finally get it done—all five stories—we should be able to house two thousand of us, maybe more. Also, these are all bare suites. Once you figure out who will live where, we'll move in the furnishings from the ship and then your belongings."

While the vast crowd departed with many talking about who could stay with who, Hanna and Ralph held back until she could talk with Raven.

"Excuse me, Miss Cooper, may I, we, have a word? I'd like to have my last name changed to Riggs. I don't want to be associated with the Stroebels ever again. And can anyone get married any longer? We want to be married somehow."

"Darn, you've pointed out another hole in our society. For sure you can be called Hanna Riggs. I'll make that change in my official roster. Since everyone looks to me for rulings, I think I've a way for you to marry. Officially."

Raven signaled Faith, escorting the last of the visitors out of the castle.

"You're the ship's commander now, more or less, right?"

"Well, yes, but the ship's about kaput. Why?"

"Commanders have the authority to marry people. Right?"

"Yes, why?"

"Well, Hanna and Ralph want to be married now."

"Cool. But don't you want a ceremony or something?"

"No. Just make us officially married so we can always live together. Just we want to do it now, before all the picking of suites happens."

"Ah, ha. Now that makes sense. Ace, come over here. You and Raven are the witnesses. Hanna, do you take Ralph to be your lawful wedded husband? Oh, I'm supposed to say in sickness and in health."

Hanna grinned. "I do."

After Ralph said his words, Faith said, "I now pronounce you man and wife. You may kiss the bride."

Both flushed, but they exchanged a passionate kiss.

Raven said, "I'll make the notations in the group's ledger now. Are you going to discuss sharing a suite with your parents?"

Ralph's face crimsoned. "I can now. If they don't want us, then we'll apply for one of those tiny closet suites. It's at least as big as Hanna's cabin now."

With his arm around Hanna, Ralph led them off to visit his parents, Basil and Lyn Riggs. They found the Riggs' clan meeting in his uncle's suite. The discussions ceased as the pair walked in. Many eyes stared at Hanna.

"Mom, Dad, this is Hanna Riggs. We just got married. The XO did it. Please don't get upset. We love each other."

"So this is where you've been spending all your time, is it? With her?" Lyn said, a big grin spreading. "Congratulations, Hanna. Welcome to the Riggs clan. That's his father, Basil. His younger sister, Judy."

"Hi. I'm Uncle Henry, my wife, Scarlet. Our sons, Tom and Phil."

"Very pleased to meet all of you."

"We're thankful for your help in the gardens," Lyn said. "Is Ralph helping you enough?"

"He's saved my life, if I'm honest. He's brilliant. Yes, I've been a brat, but I simply must learn to be a valuable member of our country. I won't be a burden on you."

"No, she's the greatest woman in our world," Ralph said. "But we'd rather not live in one of those closet cabins. Are all of you planning to move into one of the larger suites?"

"That's just what we were discussing. There are only seven of us, er, nine of us. Either we take one of the smaller suites or we get others to join with us," Basil said.

"Can't we ask the Norton's?" asked Tom. Phil nodded vigorously.

"Please," Judy added.

Basil and Henry headed off to check with the Norton family.

Ralph whispered to Hanna, "Tom and Phil really like their daughters, Sabrina and Poppy, while Judy has her eyes on Elmo."

"Well, there aren't that many their own ages around here," Hanna whispered back.

"Tea anyone?" Lyn asked.

"Yeah, thanks," Hanna grinned.

"Okay. You'll forgive us for being so—well, I don't know. So nervous around you. We don't know what we should or should not do. Our Ralph is so grownup."

Ralph said, "Treat her like Judy."

Over tea, Judy sat beside Hanna so she could whisper to her. "I'm dying to know. Have you been able to sleep with him? Ralph? He's always been terribly shy around girls."

"He's not anymore," she winked. "He's incredible in bed. How about you and Elmo?"

She giggled. "We've tried, but folks say we're too young for that. Wait another year, Mom says. How did you get married?"

"We asked Raven who had XO Faith Koralsky marry us. She's a ship's commander who can marry people."

The men returned with the five Nortons. After some discussion and begging from the teens, Norton and Riggs agreed to share one of the larger sized suites, but might fit into a middle sized suite if needed. The men headed off to find Raven and make their request. While Hanna and Ralph wanted to return to her tiny cabin, the others wanted to know all about the pair and how they married.

Hanna told them what she thought they could accept and without sharing her deepest feelings. I opened my eighteenth birthday present from my mother, who died when I was five. Whatever the present was, it brought back awful memories. Ralph was there to save me."

A week later, these families got the go-ahead to move in. First workers ripped out carpeting in their various quarters and placed them in their new suite, Number 1-2-1. Next, all beds and linens were boxed up, moved, and reassembled. Hanna and Ralph had the smallest side bedroom of the suite. Then workers moved their personal possessions, including wardrobes and cabinets, tables, and chairs.

To make things easier for Hanna, Ralph put all her things in the top two drawers of the cabinet. That done, the pair made a last trip to their cabins on the spaceship, double checking that nothing had been left behind.

"This is a finality, isn't it?" she said, staring at her empty cabin. "We'll never see this again."

"Yeah, I think they'll continue to cannibalize the ship, especially once there's no functioning life support systems. Kind of sad. Leaving the ship behind. An ending. We're not being rescued or calling for help."

Hanna sighed, then said, "Yes. Initially, I prayed for someone to rescue me from this desolate planet and these crazy people. Now, being here with you, I don't want to leave. How weird is that?"

"Not strange at all. We found love. I'll never leave you. I'll follow you wherever you go. You can't get rid of me."

Hanna grinned. "You can't get rid of me either."

With the move completed and the first ice storm of the season raging outside the orange granite walls, Raven used the new intercom system they'd cannibalized from the ship. "Okay. This is our new system. I have two announcements. First, our doctors have asked me to tell you we have used up the contraceptive supplies. Second, based on that, all restrictions on who can have a baby are lifted. Just try to have as many different fathers as possible to keep our limited gene pool as broad as possible. Third, I'm holding a surprise party for Ace to thank him for making our castle. Food and drinks are on me in the dining room. Oh, fourth, the new sickbay is now in Suite 1-1-1. Can't miss it. Fifth, if you plan on getting pregnant, please see our doctors for a quick checkup. Bye."

Chapter 23 Baby Boom

After getting moved into their new sickbay, Dr. Wu and Dr. Johnson met with Raven. Dr. Wu said, "We're out of contraceptives. We have limited ability to abort fetuses who are malformed or in order to save the woman's life. Yet, we know our society needs many more babies for it to survive. We're bound to lose a few women to this. And what happens later on once we doctors are gone? How will women get the pregnancy care they need, let alone assistance with birthing?"

Raven sighed. "Been expecting this to raise it's head. My best suggestion is to begin training midwives to help out. If you get Hanna Riggs trained up, since she's young, she'll be able to help for decades, long after you are gone. My suggestion is get as many young women trained up as best you can."

***

Additional problems arose at once. No running water and no showers.

Hanna said, "We have a problem, honey. How do we shower? How do we get a drink? How do I handle going in a chamber pot? What about soap? Washing my hair? Wow! Washing our clothes. Has anyone thought about these necessities? God, no hot water either. Am I supposed to go the well to fetch water?"

From the adjacent room, they heard Judy calling out. "Mom, there's no running water. How do we take showers? No hot water either. How am I supposed to wash my clothes? Mom?"

A minute later, everyone in the suite met in the common room, discussing these issues. Hanna felt relief that she wasn't the only one baffled by the sudden changes demanded of them.

"We've taken life's simple things for granted," Hanna said. Most nodded. "So, how do we do these things?"

Lyn said, "We've got a large wooden barrel over there. I guess we fill it with water and wash clothes in it. Maybe. Where do we dump the dirty water? Wait. The bucket we use to draw water only holds a gallon. This tub will take at least twenty bucket loads. Maybe we're supposed to only take sponge baths in the winter. Perhaps in the summer, we can bathe in the river and wash laundry there, too."

Raven and Faith also faced the same problem the first morning they woke in their new suite. Using the new comm system, Raven called for a meeting in the dining room while they ate breakfast, which became delayed for similar reasons.

"Look, we overlooked a few things. Without the ship and its hot water system, we face no showers. And as Hanna pointed out to me minutes ago, how do we wash clothes? The wells provide about a gallon of water at a time. So here's my plan. We still have plenty of copper ore. Let's organize crews to convert copper into caldrons that can hold enough water for one person to bathe in or wash clothes in. Ace says the chamber pot waste disposal system is where we can also dump dirty water. Since each suite has a coal fireplace, you can heat water there. Yes, it's going to take the most getting used to that we've yet faced.

"After we've adapted a bit, come spring, I have some ideas we can use to make our own castle running water system, using piping from the ship. We'll have to wait until the snows have melted to salvage that. I know this isn't what you wanted to hear. But remember the old saying, 'Rome wasn't built in a day.' By this time next year, every suite will have running water. Trust me on this."

After she finished, Ace asked, "How can we have running water?"

"Put a water tower on each floor. But we'll need some kind of pump system to fill them up. If we make their capacity large enough, we'll only need to man the pumps maybe once a week. Hans, you get to design the pumps. Perhaps use horses or caribou or humans to provide the horsepower."

Hanna overheard this and said, "I have an idea. Since we're cannibalizing the ship, why not take a lot of the aluminum walls and such and form them into giant water containers, like water towers? Then have a coal fire burning under one and use it to make the hot water. Of course, someone would have to stoke the fires daily."

"Brilliant," Hans said. "She's right. This we can do. Should have thought of this long ago."

"But we were still living on the ship," Hanna said.

"Precisely," Raven said. "This is one of those last-minute duh's that sometimes happens.'

"We can reuse all the fixtures in our showers and bathrooms, too," Hanna added.

"Let's sit down and discuss this further, Hanna. Excellent ideas," Hans said.

Within a day, people worked out systems to handle their water needs. Fetching water became a morning chore assigned to one member of each suite. They filled up the twenty-gallon containers in the suites. Another got assigned to collect and dump all the chamber pots. Soon, everyone took to dumping a bucket down the system after the last of the pots had been emptied, which reduced some of the odor.

Hanna and Ralph continued handling the dirty dishes for the chef, though now they no longer had the fancy dishwashing machines. Ralph got the 'dirty job' and she continued rinsing and drying the many metal dishes and silverware.

***

As the winter progressed, many women visited the doctors to have them check on the new pregnancies. Hanna visited Dr. Wu.

"I'm nauseous in the morning, and I missed my period, which is a good thing, since we are out of feminine products."

"Yes, that's going to be a problem for you women. Let's check you out. Blood pressure is fine. I hear a heartbeat. Come back next month, but come at once if you experience anything unusual. We doctors are now flying blind, as Ace would say. Lost all our fancy medical equipment."

As spring came, fifty-three women were expecting. Fortunately, only twice did two women give birth on the same day.

These winter months challenged Hanna. So many things she could no longer do, which she used to do in her cabin on the ship. Ralph never let her dwell on this for long. Near the end of her pregnancy, she needed his help with almost everything.

"I'm a blimp. A bloated blimp."

"You're going to be a wonderful mother," he countered.

Then the day they'd been waiting for came. Ralph, frantic with worry, carried her to the sickbay suite. Neither knew what to expect. Lyn arrived just after the pair.

"Son, this is a job for us women. Go sit out in the common room. I'll look after Hanna now."

Dr. Wu washed his hands in the cold water, grimacing. "Hope you get your hot water system going soon, Hanna. Can you tell me what you and Hans are planning?"

By now, he had learned the best way to deal with panicking women in labor was to distract them. And he had developed a knack for this by knowing his patients. He kept asking her for more details while Lyn mopped Hanna's head and his nurse kept watch. The baby slipped out before Hanna realized it was coming.

"Ah, there you go. You have a wonderful daughter, Hanna. She's going to look a lot like you. A beautiful girl. See?" He held her up so she could see while the nurse brought in hot water to wash the baby off. Lyn prepared a diaper and the baby clothes that Judy had worn many years ago.

"Does she have all her fingers and toes?" Hanna asked. "We hoped she would, Dr. Wu. She's so tiny. Are all babies this tiny?"

Lyn grinned. "Hanna, your baby's weight is above

average. Looks like you are going to have big babies. Have you and Ralph picked out a name yet?"

"Ilse, after my mother. If it was a boy, we picked Bart after his grandfather. Boy, do I ever have so many new things to learn how to do!"

Ralph joined them and got to hold Ilse. "She's beautiful, just like her mother."

When they were alone, she said, "I don't know anything about caring for a baby. And now I really need your help."

"Like always, we'll figure it out together," he said.

By the end of summer, fifty-three babies increased the population to well over seven hundred, which was an encouraging sign that Raven pointed out to everyone.

Chapter 24 The End

I'm looking at my birthday cake. White, with Raven in red frosting. I'm now eighty-two years old. Well, sort of. When I first came to Landfall, I was twenty-two Earth years old. Here, a year is four hundred days long. But then a day is twenty hours long. Long ago, following my advice, we tracked time using Landfall units. After the third year here, the spaceship ceased functioning, so we lost all ways of tracking Earth time. I feel so old, so tired, and my insides hurt.

Dr. Wu passed away two years ago, and Dr. Johnson can still get around, almost. Without medical machines, he cannot diagnose what's wrong with my body, let alone heal it. I know it's dying. We all do.

My oldest, Rose, promised to help me take a walk outside Cooper Castle. They named it after me, and I suppose they felt the need to honor me. All these years, I've been their guiding light, their leader, the one person who always made the right decisions for us to survive and prosper.

Ace built this orange granite castle to shelter us from the harsh winters of Landfall. His plan called for five stories, four towers, a gatehouse, and many spires. I can walk, but only with help. Each slow step feels like my insides are tearing apart. But I want to see the castle proper one more time. Rose understands.

The chilly air no longer bothers me, as I stand gazing at the main entrance of the giant castle. The towers glow in the noon yellow sun. And the noise and odors floating in the air are a testimony to all I've worked for my entire adult life. With my guidance, Coopertown has grown, becoming the largest town on Landfall. While the other four groups went their own ways, none of them can boast the splendor of our town.

Horses, chickens, sheep, caribou, and cows are

thriving in the spring-growing grasses in the stone-lined fenced-in areas beyond the castle. Nearby, workers are preparing the gardens for planting this season. Our gardens now span forty acres, but the grain fields have exploded to several square miles. They continue to follow my original suggestion, which was each year double the size of the gardens and fields. Why so much? Trading with the other four groups. We need the wool from the Scotts, horses from the Spaniards, cattle and honey from the Basques, and iron items from the Germans. And we get vast loads of nuts from all four. I suspect one day these groups will finally be able to supply their own food needs.

I breathe deep before another coughing fit ends it. Rose ushers me back inside, though I am still marveling at what we've accomplished in these sixty years.

I never married. Not a fan of men that way. Funny how one experience when you're young influences your life, but it did. My best friend and partner, XO Faith Koralsky, passed away last year. But she and I did our part, bearing four children each. Early on, I worked out a population progression for our survival. When the reality of us being stranded forever on this desolate world finally struck, some committed suicide. I wanted the rest to have a future and hope. Hence my population studies.

Each woman needed to produce four children. Our children next had to create at least three each. After that, normal birth rates would suffice. Trouble was, we ran out of contraceptives. Even worse, we ran out of hygiene products for us menstruating women. Talk about a grand mess. Anyway, during these sixty years, many women had more children than I'd planned. And that proved a good thing, because I neglected deaths during childbirth and infant deaths in a primitive society. Which shows I can make mistakes like everyone else.

And my biggest mistake was forgetting how we'd have water in our suites when we first moved into the castle. Ace had the foresight to make a well at the end of each hallway on the first floor. But I forgot about showers, sinks, and clothes washing. And they let me know that problem the day after we moved into the suites on the first floor.

Thanks to Hanna and Hans, my oversight got remedied fast. And today, each floor has its own water tanks. Metal salvaged from the ship. Below one is a coal-fired furnace, heating all the water in that tank. Gravity forces the water down pipes into each bathroom and sink in each suite, controlled by faucets and showerhead confiscated from the cabins in the spaceship. On each floor, we assign one person to attend the coal fire each day. And a team on each floor mans the water pumps when either tower runs low. We did it this way, floor by floor, since the construction of each new floor took years of work, more so when the power packs died and Ace couldn't recharge his many disintegrator guns he'd been using to carve the granite blocks for the castle walls.

We still maintain the hand-cranked communication units, one in each of the five groups. A comm operator has a specific schedule she maintains. By cranking the unit, it powers up for a few minutes. Beside her desk and comm system, she has posted a month calendar on which day which group might call us. That system came compliments of XO Koralsky. And sixty years later, it's still our only easy way to stay in touch with the various groups.

Yes, overland traders are now quite the thing, coming at all times after the spring thaws. But thousands of miles separate each of the five groups. And the five shuttles from the cruiser have long ceased flying, having used up all the fuel on the cruiser. I remember that first spring when desperate men from each of the other four groups came to trade for critically needed supplies. And now traders come every week, some making their rounds from one group to the next, never staying in one place, except during the winters.

They cut my birthday cake while Rose helped me sit at the table. My clan gathered around me, my four children, my twelve grandchildren, and my six-so-far great-grandchildren. And their spouses or significant others, too. I tried to eat a bite, the red R, but that was all I could manage before another coughing fit seized me. I must have blacked out.

I woke lying in my bed, the bed I had shared all these years with Faith Koralsky. No, we were not lovers in the way you must think. Rather, more like the sisters we never had. The bestest of best friends, inseparable, until death took her from me. One by one, the clan tip-toed in to look at me, afraid noise might hasten my death. Such strange thoughts.

At least no one asked me how I was feeling. Perhaps I had Rose to thank for that. Her gift blended with her passion for nursing. She could sense what the ill or injured person needed, an invaluable skill for her, especially when our two real medical doctors could no longer be effective.

Gifts. Yes, that's what the doctors and I call them. More than half of our original group developed some form of it. We think the greatly enlarged pituitary glands, which doubled or tripled in size, caused it. Those who didn't get a gift still had normal sized glands. Admittedly, after the ship's power supply died during our third year, the doctors could no longer do a scan to check on the gland's size. But we still kept records of the gifts people received. To this day, we're uncertain what caused the gland's explosive growth, but we tied our theory to the abundance of that whitish organic phosphorous substance sent into the air from the zillions of yellow buttercup-type spring flowers.

Cooper Castle was the grand vision of Ace. How to cut up the sod and make mud bricks was Lyn's vision. Hanna's visions allowed us to reuse the extensive water system of the cruiser. And the list goes on and on. The gifts appear to be visions or imaginations which, if followed, lead to valuable results. It's not as though the recipient has magical powers, but more like an instinctive intuition about how to do something, to remedy something, how to fix something, or how best to deal with something.

But then, none of this could be the truth. Hanna, for example, bucks this theory. Her gift is very rare and is a closely guarded secret known only to five people, including herself and her husband. I'm one of those select people, as was Faith. Now the new head of security also knows. Hanna can read a person's surface thoughts. Why a secret? If others knew she could read their minds, well, I leave it to your imagination. But it wouldn't be pleasant for Hanna.

My body feels stiff now. And cold. I think I'm dead. There are all my kids standing around my bed crying. Wait. Someone's with me.

'Yes, I'm with you. It's me, Hanna. I've chosen to let you in, my way of thanking you for all you've done for all of us.'

'So intimate. Am I in your mind?'

'Yes. I've only let a very few people in here with me. Ralph and our children. Now you. This is what it's been like for Ralph and me all these years. A closeness beyond description.'

'Is my body dead?'

'That's what they're saying. Can you hear the bell tolling? Rose ordered it to sound on your death to let everyone know. I've got to go now. Again, thank you for everything.'

But I'm dead. And still can think. Oh, I see my body down there. The bell. Yes, I hear it now. How is this possible? Where are they carrying my body? Ah, into the spacious rotunda beneath the top tower. My goodness. Look at that line of people. What are they looking at? Oh, my body. So many tears. How long is that line? Hundreds and hundreds. I recognize many of them. Students. I taught them calculus and physics. Is the entire Coopertown walking by my body? Someone's posting a sign. What's it say? The Guardian Goddess Angel of Coopertown. I'm not an angel or a goddess. Rose is saying something.

"Goodbye Mom. You're the absolute best mother anyone could ever have. We'll all miss you."

You can stop crying now, dear. I'm alright. I'm not dead. Well, my body is dead, but I'm not my body. I never knew that. I wonder if anyone ever figured this out.

Wait. What do I do now? Where do I go? I still don't

know where Earth is at, so I can't go there, and I have no spaceship to go in. But do I need a spaceship to go anywhere?

And look at all those pregnant women filing by. Maybe I can get one of their new baby bodies somehow. Yes, I've an image of Mom. I'm swooping down and latching onto her baby right after it's born. Hey, bright idea. I can pick my new mother this time. Who shall it be? But maybe a long rest is in order. I feel tired. I could use a very long nap.

The one thing I didn't work out was who will take my place. Everyone looked to me and Koralsky for guidance. What will they do now? My guess is they'll elect a king and queen, because that's much simpler than setting up a democracy. Faith thought we should have set up a system of government. It's just that we could never decide on what form it should have.

I know what I want to do now. Go find Faith. I miss her so much. Did she get a new baby body? I wonder how I can find her. How will I recognize her? Will she recognize me? This is intriguing. I'm thinking, but I'm dead. Or rather, my body is dead. How is this possible? Am I an angel, after all?

The End

A Favor to Other Readers

How about helping other readers? Many readers rely on reviews to make the decision whether to buy a book. You can help them make their decision by leaving your opinions and viewpoint in a short review of the positive things of this book. Writing the review and expressing your opinion only takes a few minutes, and other readers will appreciate your efforts.

Author Information

Visit My Amazon.com Author Page
Vic Broquard Author Page

Follow My Blog
Vic Broquard's Blog

Follow Me on Social Media

Facebook

LinkedIn

YouTube

Other Books by Vic Broquard

Without Warning (fantasy)

The Trident Series: (fantasy)

- Volume 1 The Trident and the Book
- Volume 2 The Trident and the Scepter
- Volume 3 The Trident and the Resurrection

The Adventures of Elizabeth Stanton Series: (science fiction)

Volume 1 The Evolution of the Path
Volume 2 The Great Messiah
Volume 3 Of Kings and Queens and Troubadours
Volume 4 Chaos in the Aftermath
Volume 5 Power Plays
Volume 6 Age of Exploration
Volume 7 Abducted
Volume 8 The Emperor and Empress
Volume 9 A Job Worth Doing
Volume 10 Degradation
Volume 11 The Second Crusade
Volume 12 When Worlds Collide
Volume 13 Dark Ages

The Lindsey Barron Series: (fantasy)

Volume 1 The Rod of the Apocalypse
Volume 2 The Board of Governors
Volume 3 The Crown of Moses
Volume 4 Dominus for President
Volume 5 The National Health Care Program
Volume 6 States Justice
Volume 7 Cross and Double-cross
Volume 8 Down the Dragon Hole

Zoran Chronicles Series: (fantasy)

Volume 1 A Dragon in Our Town
Volume 2 Dragons, Power, Courts, and War

Planet of the Orange-red Sun Series: (science fiction)

Volume 1 When Kingdoms Fall
Volume 2 Dark Ages
Volume 3 Age of the Towers
Volume 4 Difficillis Exitus
Volume 5 Age of the Lords
Volume 6 The Renegade Tower
Volume 7 Rebellions
Volume 8 The Aliens Return

Volume 9 Power Struggles
Volume 10 Guilds, Genetics, and Gods
Volume 11 Magi, Witches, Swords, and Superstitions
Volume 12 The Voyage of the Eagle's Seed
Volume 13 Eagle's Seed and Origins
Volume 14 Justifications
Volume 15 Responsibilities

The Return of the Wizards: Twelve Companions – The Making of Wizards (fantasy)

Slow Comes the Dark Series: (science fiction)
Volume 1 Creeping Darkness
Volume 2 Serendipity
Volume 3 Darkness Descends
Volume 4 Perversion Incarnate
Volume 5 Extermination Wars

Reclamation Series: (science fiction)
Volume 1 For the Want of a Pill
Volume 2 Organ Donors

Dragons, Magic, and Me Series (fantasy)
Volume 1 The Box

The Sol Empire (science fiction)
Volume 1 For the Want of Humanity
Volume 2 Fear
Volume 3 Greed
Volume 4 Power Moves
Volume 5 Genetic Engineering
Volume 6 Religion and Robots
Volume 7 Telepath Nightmares
Volume 8 Origins

AI Bureaucracy (science fiction)
Volume 1 The Algorithmic Trap

Landfall (science fiction)

Landfall Volume 1 Survival

www.ingramcontent.com/pod-product-compliance
Lightning Source LLC
Chambersburg PA
CBHW061549250926
52052CB00010B/3135

* 9 7 8 1 9 4 1 4 1 5 9 1 7 *